This book is a work of fiction. Names, characters, places, and incidents are either the product of the author's imagination or are used fictitiously. Any resemblance to actual persons, living or dead, events, or locales is entirely coincidental.

The following story contains mature themes, strong language and sexual situations. It is intended for mature readers.

All characters are 18+ years of age and non-blood related, and all sexual acts are consensual.

Lauren Landish

## Table of Contents

## Introduction

**Make sure to join my mailing list to be notified of new releases and for giveaways! You will not be spammed and your information will never be given or sold. You can unsubscribe at any time.**

**Lauren Landish Mailing List**

**Connect with me on Facebook. I love hearing from readers. Don't be shy!**

**View my entire catalog on my Amazon Author Page.**

\* \* \*

**She's Daddy's little girl, but I'll make her a rebel.**

They call me a killer—a felon. I spent five years in a medium security sh\*thole.

I swore I'd stay out of trouble, but when I met Abby Rawlings, all bets were off. From the moment I laid eyes on her, I knew I had to have her.

But Daddy dearest is standing in my way. He thinks I'm no good for her, and he's declared her Off Limits.

Well, I don't give a damn. In the end, I'll make her mine.

## Chapter 1

## Abby


"And so, as our country faces the challenges of a new generation, it's still important for us to remember the values that brought us here. Hard work. Family. And most of all, our faith, both in each other and in God."

I tried not to sigh too much. I knew that it wasn't what Daddy would want. I hated this sort of political stuff, especially since I thought that the man speaking had absolutely no idea how to lead a dog pound, let alone a higher office. Still, my sigh caught Brittany's attention. She leaned over to whisper in my ear. "Abigail, come now. Try not to fidget so much."

"Brittany, nobody's paying attention to me. Everyone's paying attention to Greg," I replied, also keeping my voice low. I may not have wanted to be there, but I still was doing my best to respect Daddy's wishes. "He's the man of the hour."

"Still, people are going to look. And I've asked you before; in public, please call me Mother," Brittany said. Actually, she wasn't my real mother. Brittany Worthington-Rawlings had married my father when I was thirteen years old. After his first marriage was cut short by a traffic accident that took both my mother and my older sister's lives when I was three, Patrick Rawlings had raised me by himself for nearly eight years before marrying again—this time not so much for love, but for what could best be termed *advantage*. Tired of working so hard and still being stiffed by those in established families with society connections, Daddy married Brittany Worthington. From one of the long-established families in Atlanta, she'd fallen on hard times financially when her first husband had been convicted of insider trading and sentenced to five years in jail. She hadn't signed any sort of prenuptial, so their bank accounts and estate were considered one by the IRS and the SEC, which cleaned her and her family's hundred-year-old fortune out to the tune of tens of millions of dollars.

She hadn't exactly been living on the streets. People from Brittany's roots don't end up on the streets, but she had been forced into societal situations that she didn't want to be in, such as not going to the Master's Gold Tournament because she couldn't afford to be even a basic patron.

For both of them, the marriage had been advantageous. At first, I'd been quietly opposed, because my daddy shouldn't marry for anything but the most noble of intentions. I'd held my tongue, however, and I had to admit that as the years went on, they did seem to care for each other, even if there was never quite the amount of tenderness and affection I had seen in the old home videos of Daddy and Mom. Of course, both also got what they wanted, too. Daddy got access to the society connections that had eluded him for years, and Brittany got access to Daddy's bank account, free and clear of the government.

But, it never really seemed like she wanted to be the mother to a nearly teenage girl, and for that, she and I didn't really get along all that well. She never went to any of my school events, parent teacher conferences or anything of the sort. The only time my presence was really important was when she wanted me to grow into a young society woman that she could mold into the image she wanted. It was the last thing I wanted, but there wasn't much I could do about it.

Around the house, at least, we could avoid each other as we were three people living in a house that had five bedrooms along with ten acres of property. As long as we weren't in public, that suited both of us just fine. On the positive side, though, Daddy still kept a bit of his blue collar roots, and at least at home, he didn't mind if I acted like a bit of a tomboy. I could wear shorts and t-shirts and go hang out in the back yard however I wanted. On the weekends or when he had free time, Daddy and I would go riding our ATV's, go fishing at the river that ran through the back of the property, and all sorts of things that we both enjoyed.

In public, though, he let Brittany have a much freer hand in her critiques of how I acted. "Honey, I spent too many years breaking my back because too many people around these here parts still think who you know is more important than what you know. They'd let me build their houses, their office buildings, hell, even their country clubs, and they never let me inside, no matter how much money I had. These people have ways of doing things that I don't know, or perhaps I do, but I know that there's no way I could get through those ways on my own. Brittany does know, and she can get through, and I want you to learn from her. Because I'll be damned if I'm going to let my daughter scrap and scrape the way I had to before you were born."

Regardless of the reason for his thoughts, Daddy didn't say anything as Brittany corrected me for the tenth time that night. At least I didn't have a stepbrother or stepsister to go along with the whole deal, a sibling who would know all of the rules that I didn't—or did know

7

but didn't want to follow. There was nobody my age, at least, to give me the hairy eyeball. That would have been too much.

"Abigail, you must learn the most basic lesson. In public, you're always being watched, and you must always be watching as well," Brittany whispered, continuing her lesson. "For example, did you notice that Henrietta DeKalb has already drunk four glasses of wine during her husband's speech?"

Henrietta DeKalb, wife of Gregory DeKalb, was one of Brittany's frequent points of observation. There seemed to be some sort of long-term animosity between the women, but I never quite understood what it was. For all I knew, it stretched back generations. That was the way things ran in this level of society. Still, for all of Brittany's pointed commentary, I didn't really care if Henrietta was sucking down Old English Malt Liquor straight from the bottle, or if she was primly sipping Darjeeling from a china cup. I just didn't want to be there.

Unfortunately for me, Daddy's desire to be accepted into the upper crust of central Georgia society meant I had to endure such events on a much more frequent basis than I'd have liked. This night, we got to listen as Greg DeKalb gave a campaign speech in front of the *ahem* fraternal club that both he and Daddy now belonged to. Daddy had been accepted only after his marriage to Brittany. Greg was running for Governor in the next election, and he was certainly hitting up his cronies at the club for funds. While I saw nothing wrong with trying to get money from his friends, the dog and pony show that was this speech and dinner just dragged on my nerves. Seriously, why not just go around the golf course while shooting a round and ask for support? At least then I wouldn't have to sit through it.

Thankfully, Greg's speech went on for just another few minutes before he wrapped it up, and the two hundred dollar per plate dinner started. I glanced at the ornate grandfather clock against the wall near where we were sitting, stifling a curse that certainly would have earned another rebuke from Brittany. Once the lights rose, I turned to Daddy, pointedly ignoring her. "Daddy, I understand that this is something you wanted to do, but would you mind if I go?"

"Go where, honey?" Daddy asked, reaching for his knife. Two hundred dollars was a lot of money for a steak dinner, and inwardly, I was thinking that for the price of just one of the three plates Daddy had paid for, he and I could have had a lot more fun doing something else. "Dinner just started, and if you go now, you'll miss dessert. It's supposed to be the famous bourbon vanilla pudding. Since you're over twenty-one now, I don't think it'd be too bad if you had some."

I looked down at my steak, which despite the price tag looked like something I could have gotten at Outback, and tried not to push it away. It's not that I have anything against a good steak. In fact, I'll eat just about any meat you put in front of me, but that night, I didn't want to even touch it. What I wanted to do was get out of that club.

Daddy's marriage to Brittany had certainly solved some problems for him, and I gave him credit. He didn't let it change who he was at the core. But there were still issues that I didn't like. First of all, it made Daddy even more desperate to be accepted in this upper class of Atlanta society, and as anyone who's been to high school in the past generation can tell you, the worst way to be accepted was to act desperate for acceptance. The society types begrudged Daddy a seat at their table, partly because of Brittany's connections but also because of his money. He'd built so many houses and owned enough housing subdivisions that he could have ignored them, but he didn't, probably because of his roots in the working class. He wanted to show them up and at the same time force them to accept him after they'd ignored him for so long.

But, the biggest problem I had with Daddy's marriage to Brittany was that it made his overprotective streak even more stifling. When Mom and my sister, Connie, had been killed, Daddy and I only had each other. For eight years, Daddy protected and cared for me, and I was the only girl in his life. I was all he needed, and he was all I needed. We took care of each other, like the times I'd make Kraft mac & cheese with cubed ham on the nights that he had to be at the job site late. He'd come home to a warm meal, and I'd already fed myself and cleaned up everything but his bowl, and if I was awake, I'd be either doing my homework or watching a bit of TV like a good girl should.

When Brittany came along, though, Daddy had gone from merely making sure I didn't get hurt, to letting Brittany set all sorts of rules about where I could go, what places were good enough for me, and worst of all, which people I could and could not see. She wanted me to carry on the society connections that she had given Daddy access to, including making sure I met up with the right kind of boys. Most of them were snobbish losers, and more than a few I felt even I could kick their asses. It was the biggest source of conflict within my family, and now that I was nearly twenty-three, I was sick of it.

"Daddy, one of the girls from my European history class invited me to an art exhibition, and I told her I'd go. I didn't know at the time about tonight. But if I leave now, I can meet up with her in time for the opening event," I said, trying not to put a hint of whine into my voice. I was a senior at Georgia Tech, for God's sake!

"I don't know, honey," Daddy said, looking at me worriedly. "Who is it?"

"The artist? I'm not really sure. I think it's someone from Germany," I said, blatantly avoiding the question since I already knew the reaction. I'd known Brittany long enough to practically read her mind on this subject.

"I think what Patrick wants to know is, which friend are we talking about?" Brittany asked. I didn't really like Brittany, but I didn't hate her either. She thought she was doing the right thing for me, even if she did treat it more as a duty than as a relationship. I could respect that, even if I didn't like it. I'd promised myself when I was younger that when or if I had a little girl, I would be more emotionally involved in her life than Brittany was in mine. "Is it Arianna?"

"No," I grumbled, not lying. I was raised better than that, and even if I was upset with Brittany or didn't like what she sometimes said, I wasn't going to lie, especially in front of Daddy.

"Who is it, Abby?" He asked, slicing through his steak. He dipped it in his little cup of sauce, chewing happily. Ever since his cardiac incident a few years prior, he'd been warned by his doctor to limit his red meat intake, and while he did his best, he relished opportunities like this to cut loose a little bit.

"Shawnie," I answered. Before Brittany could object, I started in on my defense. "She's really doing well, and her grades are good. We both graduate this year, and she's looking at going to grad school far away. So this may be one of the last chances the two of us have to do a social event together. Besides, the exhibition is near the bus stop, and I know that I can . . ."

"No," Brittany said, cutting me off. "Not with that girl. And certainly not after sunset. Do you know what sort of places girls like that go to?"

For the first time, my feelings drifted from annoyance toward anger. Brittany had never given Shawnie a chance for quite a few reasons. First of all, Shawnie was from the wrong part of the country, an out-of-state girl from the Sand Hill section of South Carolina. She'd grown up not just blue collar, but no collar at all, raised by her grandmother in Section Eight housing after her mother had abandoned her and her father went to jail. Second of all, Shawnie was independent, and fiercely so. She'd earned a full ride scholarship to Georgia Tech and was majoring in aeronautical engineering. It was only because she still had to take some core classes that we'd met at all, first by chance in a freshman English class, where we'd clicked despite the differences in our backgrounds, and then this year by design in European history, a core course that we'd both put off for far too long.

"Brittany, Shawnie's a good girl," I repeated, doing my best to keep calm. At least being angry took the whine out of my voice. "She's never been in trouble, and she's as smart as can be. A lot smarter than some of the people in this room, in my opinion. Besides, this exhibition is at The High. It's a high-class sort of event, it's close to campus, and it's going to be attended by a lot of the influential people."

"I'm sure Shawnie is a fine girl," Daddy said, trying to prevent a public argument between his wife and his daughter, "but your mother is right, honey. It's already after dark, and The High is in Midtown, where a lot of unsavory types go. Georgia Tech is a great school, and I'm proud that you're going there, but you have to admit that Midtown gets a little rowdy after dark. I'm sure that Shawnie wouldn't try to get you in trouble, but trouble could just find you in that part of town. I'm sorry, but the answer's no. Maybe next time."

"I'm twenty-two years old," I said, trying not to raise my voice. "I have to grow and get out on my own sometime. And I'll be with a friend. It's not like I'm saying I want to go to a frat party at Morehouse or something," I added, looking pointedly at Brittany. "Not that I couldn't be safe there as well."

"My answer's no, Abigail," Daddy said, setting his fork down and looking at me evenly. "Now sit down, and I don't want to hear about this anymore. You can go with your friend to this exhibition over the weekend or something. During the day."

Daddy never used my full name unless he was putting his foot down, and I could count on one hand the number of times he'd had to use that tone with me over the past year. Most of the time, I was Honey or Sweetie or Abby. When he called me Abigail, however, I knew not to try and change his mind anymore. He was decided. In normal instances, I would have just picked up my knife and fork and started eating my steak, trying to not gnaw at it in frustration.

This time, something was different. Perhaps it was that I was a senior. Maybe it was because I knew that my best friend had invited me, knowing that this could be the last time the two of us really had one of the social events she liked to call "opening our eyes to new possibilities." Hell, maybe it was Greg DeKalb's speech, which was so much the antithesis of what I personally believed that I couldn't stand it. In the end, I didn't know what came over me, but suddenly, I was on my feet, my purse in my hand. "No, not this time, Daddy. Shawnie's a good friend, and I'm going. Don't worry, I'll be home by eleven."

I stormed away from the table, hoping that Brittany's society training and Daddy's desire to fit in with the one percent crowd would keep them from coming after me. After all, regardless of how angry I was at them, I didn't want to hurt either of them. Still, I was going, and it would take someone physically restraining me to stop me. I may not stand up to Daddy often, but I'd inherited his stubborn streak along with his ears. In fact, he was just about the only person who could make me back down.

As upset as I was, I didn't cry. I was proud of that fact, at least, as I left the club and walked down the street. Despite being called a fraternal club, the club didn't have much fraternity to it at all, and in fact, the nearest university was over two miles away, quite a feat in a city with over thirty campuses in the area. In another place, or if it had been founded later, it might have just been called a club or a society, but since it had been founded when that sort of term mattered, fraternal club it was, and fraternal club it remained, along with a separate women's auxiliary that did teas and raised funds for charities and sharpened the knives they stuck in each other's back when the other wasn't looking.

Why these people didn't just ditch the club for membership at a country club where they could at least do some drinking or horseback riding or something to go along with their schmoozing, I never understood. Then again, most of them already belonged to at least one country club, so I guess it was a moot point. I'm in school to get my degree in biology and hopefully become a research nutritionist, not psychology.

I didn't cry, but that didn't mean I was thinking clearly about what I was doing. Walking south, I thought I was headed for the nearest MARTA rail station, but I somehow got turned around, totally missing it. Looking around, I had no idea where I was, except that I was in an area I'd never seen before. "Great, just great," I said, muttering to myself. "Now what?"

I reached into my purse, cursing when I remembered that I'd brought my tiny purse to the country club, the one that I never carried my smartphone in. It was the most socially acceptable of my handbags, which ranged from that up to the ubiquitous college student backpack that I preferred most of the time. I admit, I'm a bit of a tech geek, and the idea of playing with a six-and-a-half-inch screen just was too much fun to pass up. Unfortunately for me, my purse that had been deemed acceptable for the country club was much smaller, and I just never carried my phone in it.

So instead of being able to call Shawnie or a cab or even check where the hell I was with my phone's GPS app, I was standing around in a dress, four-inch-high heels, and a purse that contained my driver's license, my GT student ID, a Rawlings Construction credit card that I was authorized to use, and thirty-eight dollars in cash. No change, of course, since *ladies do not jingle.*

Sighing, I looked around and could see the Midtown skyline to my right. "Well, you haven't been doing all those spin classes for nothing," I said to myself, turning and walking that way. "You can make it a couple of miles, even if you are in those sexy yet sensible high heels that you just had to wear because you were hoping against the odds to meet a cute guy tonight. Although the cutest guy you've seen so far tonight is Jason Lindbergh. Ugh."

I'll admit, I have a bad habit of talking to myself when flustered, and had in fact been warned by teachers in school as I babbled answers to my tests out loud during tough finals. I'd even had to re-take my organic chemistry final in my professor's office because she said I gave half of the first section of the test away as I talked. I couldn't seem to stop it, though, and I knew that if I ever got what I wanted in life—a research lab of my own—my assistants would most likely have to wear earplugs most of the time. Maybe I'd equip them with little buzzers that I could use when I wanted their attention, although that seemed a little Pavlovian to me.

About a mile into my walk, I was more lost than ever, still not sure at all where I was, or even all that certain if I was headed in the right direction. Midtown is one of the most identifiable parts of Atlanta, but that doesn't mean the massively decentralized city doesn't have areas that make you wonder who the hell laid out the map. My ankles were starting to ache a little too, not being used to high heels. Like I said earlier, I'm a bit of a tomboy, and if that means that I go around campus at GT wearing some New Balance running shoes instead of high heels like a lot of the Southern Belles do, too bad. I still somehow seemed to attract my fair share of attention from guys, even though I wasn't all that interested in any recently. Or, to put it more precisely, I hadn't found any that were all that interesting.

In fact, it had been a while since I'd had a real date. My reputation had gotten around campus, and the fact that my father was Patrick Rawlings didn't help. I'll admit that Daddy was a bit overprotective, but he loves me, and I love him. He just had a bad habit of intimidating any of the potential boyfriends I brought home. At six foot two and still a solid two hundred and ten pounds, even in his late forties, with a work-weathered face and hands that were just as comfortable swinging a hammer as they were typing on a laptop or playing Barbie with his daughter, he scared a lot of guys off.

I was thinking too much and not really looking where I was going, but I saw Piedmont Park up ahead. Grinning, I picked up the pace despite the pain in my feet. I knew that if I made it to the park, finding The High was easy. I knew the running tracks and the sports facility layout pretty well and could easily get through the park and onto one of the major streets that would take me to The High. So I entered the park and looked for the running path, which could steer me directly to the right exit.

Unfortunately, being so focused on getting through the park, I forgot the number one rule of living in a city after dark: always keep aware of your surroundings. To hell with Brittany's rules. She'd never been downtown after dark without a security escort in her entire life. I was halfway through the park, near a little cove of trees, when two guys approached me. Both of them looked like trouble.

"Well, well, look what we've got here," one said. He was wearing Jordans and basketball gear, looking like he'd just come off the court or something, except for his bandana that was tied around his head, hiding his hair. "Hey, baby, you thinking you might need an escort through the park? It ain't safe after the sun goes down, you know."

"No, thanks. I'm fine," I said, trying to play it cool. *Don't show fear, don't show fear. They react to fear*, I kept repeating to myself. "But have a good evening anyway."

"Hey now, sweet thang," the other guy said, making me grimace at his horrible 'Dirty South' accent. "I don't think you have an option."

"I would prefer not to have your company—no offense," I repeated. I turned around and walked away from them, trying not to run. At least, not until they came after me, but they were in regular shoes, while I was wearing unfamiliar high heels and a dress. They caught up with me before I could even scream properly, pushing me off the running path and into the grove of trees nearby. As I stumbled to the ground, my left ankle twisted, and I winced even as I hit the grass.

"Get the fuck off me!" I grunted, trying not to let them get on top. One of them was trying to pin me, while the other was coming around and scanning the area to make sure we wouldn't be interrupted. I tried to scream, but the one on top of me smacked me with his right hand, rocketing my head back and bouncing it off the turf. It wasn't all that hard, but it was hard enough to momentarily stun me.

The next thing I knew, I felt his hands pushing my skirt up, and fear stabbed icily into my heart. I'd heard the statistics—most women my age have. Supposedly, one in four women my age doesn't finish college without being sexually assaulted. I'd taken all the precautions, of course: not accepting drinks from guys I didn't trust, always going buddy system to the few parties I'd attended, and stuff like that. Still, the thought that I could be one of those four never crossed my mind until that instant, and I tried to fight harder, even though I knew it was useless. The guy outweighed me by at least forty pounds and already had me pretty well pinned.

In that moment, though, just when I thought I couldn't do anything but give a good showing for myself before I was certainly beaten, most likely raped, and then killed, another man came out of the darkness, surprising the one playing lookout. I couldn't see his face very clearly. He was wearing a light hood despite the spring warmth, but I could see that he was pretty tall, and while not huge, he wasn't skinny either. He shoved the lookout into a nearby tree headfirst, his head bouncing off the tree with a rather hollow *thunking* sound, where he collapsed to the ground without even a struggle.

My near-rapist saw what happened to his companion and sprang up off me, his hands already up and swinging. He may have been skinny, but the guy was fast. He caught my unknown protector in the face with a decent punch that glanced off, following it with a kick while his back was turned. It sounded like he was wearing steel-toed boots, but the hooded man shrugged it off and kicked back with his foot, catching the guy squarely between the legs. He grabbed his very offended balls and dropped to his knees, his head thrown back and his throat making a sound something like the cross between a foghorn and a piccolo. My protector turned around and brought his right knee up in a hard arc, snapping the guy's head back and flattening him out on the ground.

The whole fight lasted fewer than ten seconds, during which I should have been scrambling to my feet and fleeing for my life. Instead,

I found myself still lying on my back, my head reeling from the whole thing, stunned not only by my attackers but by the speed of the sudden turn of events. A strange, peaceful silence dropped over the whole area, and my savior stood looking down at the body under him. Turning to me, he held out his hand. "Do you need help getting to your feet? We should go and get you looked at."

"No, I'm fine," I said, taking his hand and letting him help me up. He was strong, and he helped me up as lightly as if I'd been a small child. "Who are you?"

"Dane. Dane Bell."

## Chapter 2

## Dane

Despite the fact that it was late spring, I was wearing a hooded shirt as I walked the streets. Walking the streets seemed to be the best way I'd found to deal with the stress and uncertainty of freedom. At Leavenworth, I'd spent too much time cooped up, being told what to do, and exactly how to do it. Why was I in prison? There was a simple answer: fuck the why. Why existed for people better than me. I was a prisoner. I didn't deserve a why.

So now, freed from the confines of military prison, I walked, often for hours, starting each evening as the sun went down and sometimes lasting until midnight. As I walked, my mind would replay the frustrations of the day, driving my feet forward like an invisible mental lash. I could see in my mind the faces each time I handed my resume or application over to someone, the tightness that would come behind their eyes when they saw that I'd checked 'yes' on the box that asked if I'd ever been convicted of a felony, and the combination of fear and finality that would then come when they saw what I wrote on the line after that.

That's one of the challenges of being convicted by court-martial. If I'd been convicted of the same crime by the State of Georgia, I'd have gotten a parole officer, and the resources of said office. Now, I know it doesn't sound like much, but most parole officers know someone who knows someone who can get you a job. It may have been shoveling shit at some pig farm, but it'd be an actual job. The state system wants to at least make some sort of effort to rehabilitate its prisoners. It helps with keeping the streets safer—in theory, at least. And there's nothing wrong with shoveling shit. Someone has to do it, and I've done far worse in my years on this Earth. A lot worse.

The military justice system doesn't have that sort of backup. Once your sentence is finished and you're discharged—with, of course, the mandatory DISHONORABLE DISCHARGE stamped at the top to hang around your neck like a scarlet letter for the rest of your life— you're on your own. It was like one of the other prisoners, a former aviation captain who'd been busted for sneaking in trophies from Afghanistan and was doing a two-year stretch once told me while we played cards one afternoon:

"Uncle Sam, he's all about taking care of you when you're doing exactly what he wants you to do. Note, I didn't say do what the rules say to do, or do the right thing, but what Sam wants you do to. But as soon as you don't, Uncle Sam turns into Uncle Scrooge, and he doesn't give a fuck about you. Hell, look at the VA system. They fuck the guys who actually did good over so bad it's a fucking crime. How does that bode for us, the rejected stepchildren of Sam's brood? Bell, most of us? We've got no chance. No chance in hell once we get outside. That is, unless you want to be a mercenary. There's always someone out there with money and a need for those."

I knew all I wanted was a chance, and I didn't want to be a hired gun either. Open the door a crack, and I'd kick it in the rest of the way and show whoever gave me that chance what I could do. Hell, I was at the point where I'd take anything. Garbage man, toilet scrubber, dishwasher, greeter at Wal-Mart, anything. Still, nearly three months after being released, all I had was a growing list of rejections. I can't even say rejection letters. I didn't warrant one of those. Just rejections, usually by silence. Those were the more polite ones. There were a few who sent me on my way with choice words.

So I walked. It was cheap, and it helped the tension flow out until I could manage it enough to go back to the apartment and go to sleep, at least semi-fitfully, until five in the morning, when the dreams and nightmares would drive me out of bed, shivering and sweating despite the air conditioning that I kept cranked up to nearly frigid levels. Forty-five minutes of calisthenics and a shower before six thirty, and at seven o'clock I'd start the whole damn thing over, seven days a week. Well, except on Sundays. A lot of businesses didn't open early on Sundays, so I started my job hunting at ten in the morning instead.

I wore a hood whenever I wasn't job hunting because, despite the fact that the headlines had faded away and the chances were small, Atlanta was a military-friendly city in a military-friendly part of the country. Trainees coming to and leaving Fort Benning came in and out of Atlanta-Hartsfield airport nearly every day, escorted by their drill sergeants, some of whom were my age. These kids would get a day or two of leave if they could, and a lot of the other military members in the area would also come to Atlanta whenever they could.

It made sense for a solider. Sure, Benning had a fine military town surrounding it, and for your average run of the mill distraction, that was fine, but Atlanta was the big city, with lots to do. So between that and the former military population of the city, there were enough people. The chances of my being recognized were just too damn high. I didn't need that sort of trouble. If I'd had another option, I would have lived someplace else, but my only lifeline was in Atlanta, so I stayed and looked for work. Still, I wore a hood until my hair grew out long enough that I didn't look ex-military. Unfortunately for me, my hair grows pretty slowly, and after three months, I still looked a lot like a soldier.

As for my walking, I liked walking through Piedmont Park for a couple of reasons. Primarily, because it's green. Between the nearly uniform brown of Iraq and the gray of Leavenworth, I hadn't seen enough green in the past five years, and Piedmont gave me a chance to catch up. The lakes, the wide open grassy areas—all of it was comfortably far from my past. Secondly, Piedmont was conveniently less than a half-mile from the apartment I was using. I could use it day or night—until eleven PM, at least—rain or shine. The one day I'd taken to relax, I could even use a fishing pole I'd found in the apartment and go fishing in the lake there. I'd caught two largemouth bass before noon and ate like a king.

The night that changed my life, though, I was walking through Piedmont Park because I was, quite frankly, despondent as all hell. I'd reached a milestone that day . . . rejection number two hundred. A perfect score. Two hundred applications, two hundred rejections. That's not even counting the people who didn't reply when I put in applications online. I'd lost count of those long ago. But two hundred times, I'd walked into an office, a store, or somewhere else with my head held high, trying to ask for a chance, and two hundred times, I'd been told no. About the only option left was to go to the Day Labor office, or maybe sit outside Home Depot with the homeless and illegal aliens who depended on under the table work to make it day to day.

# Off Limits: A Bad Boy Romance

At least I wasn't homeless yet, I thought as I walked. Christopher Lake may have been an asshole, like a lot of people I knew from the military, but he was still my friend. The best friend I had, in fact. More importantly in the immediate sense, Chris was willing to let me crash at his apartment until he got back into town in a week. He'd even left me some money to help me get by and a fully stocked set of cupboards in the apartment. It had saved me more than once. I owed him everything and would always be grateful for that. Still, he was coming back from Europe in a week, and I was living in a studio apartment. What I was going to do after he got back, I had no fucking idea.

Concerns about my potential future homelessness vanished when I saw the two men dragging the girl into the tree line. Piedmont Park is dotted all over the place with these little mini groups of trees, not enough during the day to really hide what you're doing, but a good place to sit down and have a picnic or get out of the sun if you wanted to. At night, however, they provided just enough cover for all sorts of nefarious activities. My time in Leavenworth had made me pretty *laissez-faire* about the whole thing, but when I saw that, I reacted. Memories started to flash through my brain about what had gotten me into the mess I was in, and my hands balled into fists. *Not again*, I said to myself.

Thankfully, the skills I'd learned in the military hadn't faded during my years in Leavenworth. If anything, they were sharper than ever, as some of the most skilled combatants I met had a problem following orders once off the battlefield. We'd shared ideas and sometimes even trained in the dim lights and the scattered moments when the guards weren't watching us. I was able to sneak up on the first attacker while both of them were distracted by the girl, who I had to give credit for fighting hard, despite the obvious bad odds she faced. Her hands were hooked into claws, and she was trying to fend off the guy on top of her by threatening to claw out his eyes. He backhanded her, her head bouncing off the turf just as I got close.

Even the best fighter sometimes has luck on his side, and in my case, it was the fact that the angle I hit the first guy at sent him headfirst into the trunk of a tree. He dropped, and I started to turn to the other guy, but he was quick, quicker than I thought he'd be. His fist caught me in the mouth just as I was turning, jerking my head to the side. There was a momentary flash of white-hot pain, and I was pretty sure he'd cut me, probably on the ring he was wearing on his right hand. I rolled with the punch, however, and didn't take too much damage.

He followed up the punch with a halfway decent kick that had a good amount of its power taken away by the fact that his pants were sagging damn near down around his knees. His pants bound up the extension of his hip so that all he did was turn me a bit more to the side. I went with it, kicking backward with a hard kick I'd been taught first from *la savate*, the French kicking martial art. It caught the guy square in his family jewels, dropping him before I followed up with a knee that put him to sleep. The first rule you learn in street combat is that there are no concepts of fairness or sportsmanship. The guy who goes into a street fight with codes such as chivalry or fair play will usually end up bleeding and possibly dying in the middle of the street, honorable or not. Besides, the guy had been trying to rape a girl and was wearing a metal ring, so it's not like he was deserving of a fair fight or mercy.

As I stood above his laid out body, I was breathing hard, not from the exertion, but from the rush. It had been a long time since I'd tasted combat again, and I had to admit the taste was sweeter than I wanted it to be. I'd lost myself in the haze of combat before, and I was surely damned if I did it again. And I didn't mean figuratively, either.

I turned to the girl, who was still lying on the ground. She'd taken a pretty hard shot from the guy when they were struggling on the ground, and I wasn't surprised she was still a bit dazed. It takes longer than a lot of people think to recover from a hit to the head. Reaching out to her, I tried to keep my voice calm.

I didn't tell her the bigger reason I wanted to get out of there was that I didn't want the cops involved, at least not with me around. If I could get the young woman up and out of the park, maybe she'd go to the cops on her own without dragging me into it. I didn't like my chances with the Atlanta police, regardless of whether I had the woman's statement to back me up. I just didn't trust them.

"No, I'm fine," she said, taking my hand. Her skin was smooth and flawless, and a long-repressed part of me flared at the electric tingle of her fingers in my hand. I think she felt it too, because when she spoke again, her eyes were wide and her voice had the faintest hint of a tremor, although perhaps I'd imagined it. "Who are you?"

"Dane. Dane Bell." The words were out of my mouth before I'd even thought about them, and inwardly, I started cursing myself for being a damn fool. The lights were dim. I still had my hood up. I doubted she had gotten a halfway decent look at my face. If I'd lied or just not answered, I could have disappeared into the night. But that touch . . . there was no way I'd have been able to resist that touch, even if it was just her hand in mine. It was like her fingertips cut through any defenses I had and left me totally defenseless.

"Abby Rawlings. Uh, pleased to meet you." Her voice was like honey and magnolias, the sort of Southern lilt that would've turned my knees weak even before I'd spent five years in the exclusive company of men. I'd been a sucker for it ever since the first time I heard it. I came from South Dakota, where there was plenty of accent, but nothing like a Southern girl, and especially not Abby. It was the educated type of Southern, not backwoods cracker barrel that mangled grammar to the point of incomprehension, but instead just added a velvet touch to the vowels and polished the ends of certain words. I took my hand back and stepped back, ready to run, when she reached out again for me. "Stop, please."

"I really should go," I said, looking around. I wasn't sure what scared me more: the fact that I'd just assaulted two men, or the fact that even in the deep shadows, this woman was affecting me in ways I wasn't sure I was ready for yet. I hadn't tested myself in that regard yet since being freed, and I wasn't sure if I could behave the way I needed to. "I . . . I really should."

"Please, Dane. Walk me out at least. My . . . my ankle's a bit twisted, and my feet are killing me," Abby said. The way she said 'please' was irresistible, a magnet that pulled me closer to her, unable to stop myself. "And . . . I'd feel safer too."

"You don't even know me," I replied, but my feet couldn't seem to listen to my brain. Instead of turning and taking off like a bat out of hell, I stayed where I was while she found her purse and picked it up. We walked slowly back out onto the path, looking for all the world like two people taking a pleasant evening stroll and not a potential rape victim and the man who'd just beat the hell out of her attackers. "I'm not a very good man."

"You just did the most noble thing I've ever seen someone do," Abby said simply. As I listened, I realized she was more than just a wilting flower Southern belle. This girl had some strength within her, although I suspected that she didn't know just how strong she was. There was a sort of uncertainty about it, like it was just starting to come out, or she was at least unfamiliar with speaking with men like me. "You've probably got your flaws. I know I do, but for that, I feel safe enough for you to . . . what happened to your face?"

I stopped, realizing that the light from the lamp up ahead was allowing her to see what I looked like for the first time. I reached up with my fingers and felt my face, stopping when my fingers made my right cheek sting. I'd forgotten that the guy wore a ring on his hand. "Oh. I forgot the second guy must have been wearing a ring or something. It caught my face just right. It doesn't feel like much. I'm sure it'll clean up easily enough."

"You're bleeding like a stuck pig," Abby objected, her face full of concern. "We need to get you patched up, take you to a hospital."

"I . . . I don't need a hospital. Really. I'm sure it looks a lot worse than it really is," I said. A hospital was the last place I wanted to go. A hospital would mean an explanation, and an explanation could mean involving the cops. "I'll just wash it off when I get back to the apartment. It's not that far. A little hydrogen peroxide, maybe a little

29

bit of gauze, and I'll be fine. I promise."

"No way, mister," Abby said, sudden strength and confidence blooming in her voice. If I'd thought she had hidden strength before, I'd seriously underestimated her. "That needs to be washed out better than what you can do yourself in the mirror. You sure you won't go to the hospital?"

"I'm sure," I said. "I . . . I've got my reasons."

She tilted her head, giving me a questioning expression, but she nodded after a moment. "Fine. Then take me back to your place and let me clean you up. It's the least I can do."

Again, the logical side of me, the side that reminded me that I was a dishonorably discharged former soldier with a felony on my rap sheet, screamed at me to refuse her offer. But the same light that let Abby see my face, let me see her for the first time, and that logical side kept getting drowned out more and more by the voice that told me this was the most beautiful woman I'd ever seen in my entire life. Long, dark blonde hair framed a face that looked like it was carved by the gods.

Abby was stunning, with dark blue eyes that looked like flawless sapphires sparkling in the street light that seemed to bore straight into my soul. I couldn't resist those eyes and that face even if I wanted to. "All right," I said. "Uh, the place I'm staying is only a little way away. Are you sure you don't want me to call you a cab or something?"

*Don't say yes, don't say yes,* the voice in my head that was talking not with logic but with fiery emotion pleaded. When Abby shook her head and instead reached out and took my hand again, it let loose a cheer loud enough that I was sure she could hear it, even if it was invisible and inside my skull.

"Are you all right, really?" she asked as we walked. "You winced a bit there."

"Just an unpleasant thought," I said, deflecting my real thoughts. I felt like I was back in junior high school or something, and the cute girl I'd just asked to dance had actually said yes, and I was holding her hand for the very first time. "I guess the cut stings a bit more than I thought it would."

The rest of our walk seemed to nearly float by. I barely noticed when we reached the edge of Piedmont Park and turned north toward my apartment. "You know, you really handled yourself well," Abby said as we walked. "Where'd you learn all that?"

"I was in the Army for a while," I said, trying to think of some other way to answer it. "I guess it was just one of those things you learn after a while."

"Really? How long have you been out?" she asked, giving me a dazzling smile. My heart did a few lurches, along with another part of my body that was also saying it had been a long damn time since he'd had any female attention either. It was so dazzled, in fact, that I barely even noticed the alternative meaning of her question. "I mean, you're rocking two days of beard, so I guessed you're not in service anymore."

"I'm not," I quickly said. "I was discharged three months ago."

I regained my composure with the answer, and knew I didn't want her to probe there anymore. In hoping she wouldn't talk about my military history any longer, I changed the subject. "What about you? What do you do?"

"Oh, I'm a senior at Georgia Tech," she said, as if being a

student at such a good school was nothing at all. "I'm studying biology and hoping to get into a good grad school program this fall. I'd like to go into nutrition research and food science. So I guess you're not in school, then?"

"Uh, not right at the moment," I answered, slightly ashamed. After high school, I'd messed around, mostly screwing off in college until enlisting, and had never gotten any formal degree after high school. It took my going to Leavenworth to understand the value of learning. "Oh, here we are."

The Mayfair Tower is one of the best high-rise apartment complexes in Midtown Atlanta, and the look in Abby's eye as I led her inside sent chills up and down my spine. "Wow, this place is amazing. You really live here?"

"For now," I said, unwilling to say that I was merely house sitting. I wasn't an official resident, just a guest, which is why I didn't avail myself of most of the facilities in the building. The most I'd done was sneak in a couple of workouts in the fitness center during the dead of night when no one else was around to wonder who the tattooed stranger was. I would sometimes also go down and grab the newspaper from the front desk when it was a day old, looking for the classified section. In a high rise where most of the cars were under two years old, and most of the residents I'd seen had the appearance of wearing suits that probably cost more money than I'd seen in years, it was the better choice. The less I stuck out around the place, the better, I thought. "Here, let's take the elevator."

There was a comfortable silence as we took the elevator up, and I could sense a growing tension between us. It might have been a long time since I'd seen the look, but I recognized it in Abby's eyes. She thought I was attractive, and I think she also recognized that I found her stunning as well. Still, her dress, her shoes, even her purse and the way she wore her hair screamed high class and money to me. I may have been just out of jail and I may have been growing increasingly horny, but there was no way that a girl like that ended up with a guy like me. Not long-term, at least. She might want me to give it to her one time, just so she could say she'd fucked a bad boy, but that's it.

If there was one thing that my time in the Army and my time in Leavenworth had tried to drill into me, it was that for guys like me, there were no happily ever afters. I'd been born to a hard working miner who'd tried to raise me and two siblings on just what he could dig out of the ground. And while I'd not always been the best son in the world, I'd done my best to try and make myself better. But guys like me don't get a happily ever after. We get an hourly job that breaks our back while we dream of having a bigger television to take up the corner space in the double-wide trailer that's busting our checking account every month. That was a lucky ending for guys like me. Girls like Abby Rawlings never figured into our fates. Still, I couldn't repress the little ember of hope that was burning in my chest. It was why I didn't stop, and with the way Abby looked at me, I couldn't stop either way.

"Here we are," I said when the elevator stopped. I led her down the short hallway to the door, unlocking it and holding it open for her. "It's really not much, just a studio, but it's good for me."

I knew I was downplaying things, but I didn't know what else to say. The floor plan was called a Stratford, and for the Mayfair Tower, it actually was the least expensive and smallest of the apartments or condos in the place. Who knew what the hell Chris Lake paid in yearly fees? Still, compared to the cell I'd had in Leavenworth, which I shared with another man, the condo still seemed immense to me.

"It's more than good. This is really something else," Abby said as she looked around. "What's that, a sixty-inch TV?"

"I'm not sure. I don't watch it all that much," I said. In Leavenworth, TV was one of the few means to pass the time when you were indoors, and I'd had more than my fill of it. Reading, on the other hand, I couldn't get enough of. I'd come to value the knowledge contained in books, and I found them infinitely more interesting than watching reruns of cable programs—at least those the guards thought we were cleared to view. I wished that I'd been that way back in school. "I think so though."

"Daddy and I . . ." Abby started before pausing, something causing her to grow quiet. I heard the way she said the word *Daddy*, and knew that whatever her strength was, she was still at least a bit of a daddy's girl. I just hoped that didn't come with daddy issues as well. I couldn't handle that. "It doesn't matter. Come on, let's get that cut cleaned up."

"And while we're at it, let's take a look at that ankle," I said. I watched her limp when we walked, and while it wasn't bad, I didn't want her to keep putting pressure on it. "You've been hiding it pretty well, but you were limping across the lobby. I could hear it in the sound of your high heels on the tile."

Abby smiled shyly and nodded. "Okay. Do you mind if I take them off here? I'm more comfortable barefoot anyway."

"*Mi casa es su casa,*" I said, trying to force casualness. I hoped that it would calm the raging inferno that was building inside me, growing larger and larger each second I saw her in the full light of the apartment. If I thought she was stunning in the park, in the apartment, fully illuminated in the tastefully recessed track lighting LEDs that cast a glow around the room, she was ethereal. I'd never seen a more beautiful woman in my life. Barefoot, she came up to just below my chin, and her figure still concealed underneath her dress was the sort of thing artists dreamed of. She didn't seem to notice my growing desire, however, and glanced toward the back of the studio.

"I assume your stuff is in the bathroom," Abby said, looking around, her hair tossing lightly side to side. I knew instantly that when she wasn't dressed up, she was the sort of girl who liked to keep it in a ponytail. Unfortunately for me, ponytails are a major turn on, and the idea of wrapping that spun gold hair around my fingers caused my cock to surge in my pants to nearly bursting. "Or do you want me to play hide and go seek?"

I noticed that her skin was slightly flushed, and her joke was as forced as my casualness, but still, both of us smiled and I shook my head. Maybe she was feeling it as much as I was? Fresh hope flared in my chest. "Come on."

The bathroom was just after the kitchen in the L-shaped design of the studio apartment, and I found a bottle of antiseptic spray inside the medicine cabinet after rooting around for a few seconds. "Here," I said, handing it to her. "No peroxide, but this should do."

"All right then, off with your hood," Abby said. She grinned at the slightly macabre joke, her lips curling up in the most enchanting bow I could imagine. "You're already bleeding onto it, and you need to get some cold water on that fabric or else it's going to be ruined."

An electric thrill ran through me as I let her peel my shirt up and over my head, leaving me in just my jeans and boots. Abby had turned to toss my shirt through the open door to the laundry room beyond the bathroom, so when she turned back, her startled pause when she saw my upper body for the first time actually caused me to blush. She reached toward me before pulling her hand back, suddenly realizing that she hadn't asked permission. "Wow."

I tried not to let it show that I was pleased with her unexpected compliment, but I couldn't help it.

Abby blinked and shook her head, tearing her eyes from my torso to look up at my face and taking the bottle of antiseptic in her hand. "Okay, hold still," she said, moving close enough that I could almost feel the heat of her presence against the skin of my upper body. "I'll try and be gentle."

Unfortunately for Abby, the button she'd originally taken to be a weak spray turned out to be much stronger than either of us anticipated, and the resultant shot of mist not only got my cut, but also my left eye. "Ow, shit!" I gasped, immediately closing my eye and turning around. I planted my hands on the countertop, my fingers digging into the curve made by the marble of the sink. "Fuck!"

"I . . . I'm sorry!" Abby said, her voice apologetic. I was blind and in pain, but she sounded just as hurt as I was. "God, I'm so sorry!"

"No . . . it's okay," I said, tears running down my face. "You didn't mean to, and I should've closed my eye."

"Hold still," she said, putting her hands on my shoulders. I stilled, a blissful calm almost coursing from her touch into my body, as if she were some sort of magical being. "Keep your eyes closed."

I heard the water in the sink turn on, and a minute later, the cool bliss of a wet washcloth pressed against my injured eye. "Here," I heard Abby say as she gently wiped my eye and down my cheek. "I'm so sorry, Dane. You go and save my life, and I try and repay you by blinding you."

"You didn't mean to, and you don't need to repay me," I said. The pain was lessening. I turned away from the sink and reached up, putting my hand over hers to hold the compress against my eye. Her hand didn't move though, and I could feel how close she was to me. "Just let it flush out a bit, and I'll be fine. You just surprised me, that's all."

In the silence that followed, which was now tense not because we wanted to be apart, but instead because of the unspoken desire to be closer, I could hear her breath quicken. In the reddish darkness of my still tightly shut eyes, I almost thought I could hear her heartbeat. "Dane?"

"Yes?"

"What are those tattoos for?" she asked, her free hand coming up to rest on the ink that adorned my chest and arms. "There are quite a few of them."

" I got most of them in the Army," I said, trying to remember in my mind's eye what her fingers were touching. The truth was, some of them were from before the Army, a few were in service, but a lot of the others were from my time at Leavenworth. Every prisoner has their own little way of telling the administration to fuck off, and for me, it was ink. There had been a Specialist from the 10th Mountain division locked up with me who was quite the amateur artist, even though he didn't always have access to the best supplies. "I think that one is my jump wings. The parachute, right?"

"Yeah," her voice, thick and a bit deeper, said. She was feeling it too, and I was quickly losing any resistance to wanting to pull her closer. She may have been untouchable. She may have been a bit younger than me and most likely the worst mistake since I'd permanently fucked my life up with a single act in Iraq, but if I was going to be damned, there were a lot of worse ways to go than what I wanted at that moment. "What about the others?"

I took the compress away from my eye, blinking as light returned. The first thing I saw was Abby's beautiful face, and without an instant's hesitation or reconsideration, I knew that I was going to fuck her. I pulled her closer to me, my hand coming to her waist, our lips coming together, and I happily fell into damnation again.

## Chapter 3

## Abby

When I first saw Dane in the street light, it was hard to put my finger on what exactly was so fascinating about him. Obviously, I'd been impressed that he'd come to my aid and how he'd beaten up my attackers so easily. Two-on-one fights usually end up with the one getting his ass kicked. But when the light from the streetlamp let me get more of a look under his hood, there was something more about the way he looked that excited me.

Dane was certainly handsome, but it was a dark, brooding handsomeness that I wasn't used to seeing. I'd gotten used to well-groomed, slickly laid back guys who looked like they'd never really worked a hard day's labor in their lives. They were basically weak, pretty boys, and Dane was different. Black eyebrows shaded gray eyes that looked like they could either be expressive and clear or stormy and intimidating. His face was lean, with a steely tension to his features that spoke of great strength, but his mouth was large and sensual, and even with the furrow on his cheek pulling up at one corner, expressive. His short beard made him look just a bit scruffy, but in not a bad way. He looked like the sort of man who was made for a motorcycle.

"I'm not a very good man," Dane said, and in that moment, I saw something even more appealing than his dark handsomeness. I saw introspection, and yes, a bit of a haunted soul.

I'll admit, I'm a lucky girl when it came to the looks department. A lot of it came from Mom, who I wish I had gotten to know better before she died. In looking at the old pictures of her, though, her high school and college graduation photos that Daddy still kept in the family room of the house, I looked a lot like her once you account for the change in hairstyles and fashion. My hair was a shade darker though, probably because of Daddy's influence, although I'd gotten a bit of his height too. While I'm no starter for the basketball team, Mom was so short that she was nearly a gymnast.

So with my looks, even as intimidating as Daddy is, I'd had guys compliment me. The biggest problem most of them had was that they were insecure and tried to hide it by being cocky as all get out. I'd had guys try to strut past me with their chests puffed out or try to show off their clothes or their cars like peacocks at the zoo. One look in their eyes, however, told me that they were insecure little boys trying to mask imperfection behind a cocky strut of perfection.

Dane wasn't like that at all. He was up front with his flaws, and in his eyes I saw that he was, despite his protests, more of a man than anyone I'd ever met at Georgia Tech. When we got back to his place, though, I was floored. Sure, it was a studio, but the Mayfair Tower was one of those types of places that a guy around my age would be bragging about. It was furnished tastefully, though it looked like he'd recently done a major change in decor—tomething about the way the furniture was arranged in the living area and the way the couch didn't quite jive with the impression I got of Dane on the way from the park, I think. It was like there was the real Dane, and one that maybe he'd recently left behind or something.

Most of it was the contrast between his belongings. For example, the couch that he used to separate the living room area from the bed area of the studio was real leather, and while I didn't know the designer, it looked like one of those sofas that got used in photo spreads for magazines and had price tags in the thousands of dollars. On the other hand, Dane's jeans were off the rack Old Navy, and his boots I couldn't even identify. I wondered if perhaps Dane had fallen on some hard times, or if maybe he'd come into a windfall, and that was why he hadn't bragged about his living accommodations. He led me into the bathroom, and it didn't really matter. I focused instead on the task at hand, cleaning his cheek.

"All right, off with your hood," I told him as I looked at the antiseptic spray bottle. It had a lot of hype text on it, but the important part was the 99.9% printed on the side. If something had gotten into Dane's cut that this thing couldn't kill, I would be surprised.

I wasn't really paying attention as I took his shirt and tossed it into the laundry room, but when I turned around, I couldn't help but shudder at the flush of heat that ran through me at seeing his torso. The tan that highlighted his firm muscles wasn't a frat boy tan or the tan of a guy who laid out in the sun, but the tan of a man who spent plenty of time outdoors doing labor. His muscles were the real thing, not some gym rack set built with curls and pump sets, but steely cords that knew how to do real work.

And of course, there were his tattoos. I've always had a secret attraction to good body ink, though I didn't have any myself. Daddy would have had a heart attack if I did, even a little rose or butterfly on an ankle. But Dane's body was beautiful, with complex, intertwining designs that covered most of his chest and around to his shoulders, going nearly halfway down his left forearm. Whoever had done the work was talented, because even though I could see that there were different pieces from different times in his life, they all wove together in a tapestry that flowed and looked harmoniously joined, like a visual representation of his life so far.

It was the tattoos and the impressive definition of his upper body that distracted me when I triggered the spray bottle. In hindsight, I should've sprayed the gauze pad in the first aid kit and then wiped his cut, but I wasn't thinking all that clearly. I'd meant to push the plunger slowly, giving just a little squirt of liquid onto his cheek. Instead, I pushed too hard, sending a mist of the alcohol-based cleaner right into his eye. He jerked his head back, hissing in pain. "Ow, shit!" he said as he turned around. "Fuck!"

"I . . . I'm sorry!" I replied, horrified. Here he was, being a total gentleman, and I'd nearly blinded him. I felt like crying. "God, I'm so sorry!"

He squeezed his eyes shut for a minute, his face turning red as the first tears of pain trickled out of his eyes and started to make their way down his face. Still, he maintained his composure and there wasn't a hint of anger in his words. "No . . . it's okay. You didn't know, and I should've closed my eye."

"Hold still. Keep your eyes closed."

Grabbing a washcloth from the towel bar next to the sink, I quickly wet it until it was soaking. "Here," I said, pressing it against his face and taking the opportunity to apologize. "I'm so sorry, Dane. You go and save my life, and I try and repay you by blinding you."

"You didn't mean to, and you don't need to repay me," he replied, a delicious tension in his voice. His hand came up to cover mine, and my body reacted again to his presence. His touch was just as strong as it had been the first time, and my heart sped up. I didn't even realize it as I stepped closer, until I was barely a hand's breadth away from him, close enough to smell him. He smelled like a man, clean sweat and a hint of some sort of aftershave, not the fruity type either, but a real scent. "Just let it flush out a bit and I'll be fine. You just surprised me, that's all."

I tried to keep myself under control, but it was hard with him so close. I wanted to run my hand over his chest to feel the strength in his arms and his body. Even more, I wanted to feel his hands on me, and not just covering mine. I took a deep breath to try and control myself and forced my one-track mind to think of something to say. "Dane?"

"Yes?"

"What are the tattoos for?" I asked, giving in to the temptation and tracing some of his ink. I could see that not all of it was finely done. There were a few that looked a bit amateurish, but still the work of a talented amateur. I wondered where he got them. I saw a symbol I thought I knew, a set of wings coming out from a parachute on his right shoulder. "There are quite a few of them."

" I got most of them in the Army. I think that one is my jump wings. The parachute, right?"

"Yeah. What about the others?" I rasped, unable to resist it any longer. I wanted him. Right or wrong, one-night stand or forever and a day, at that moment, the thing I needed most was his touch, his caress. I wanted to taste his skin and run my tongue along the intertwining lines of his ink. When he opened his eyes and looked down into my eyes, I knew that he wanted it too.

His hands pulled on the backs of my arms, and I wouldn't have been able to resist even if I wanted to as he brought my lips to his. His mouth was as supple and amazing as I'd been imagining, his lips sending shivers down my spine even before his tongue came out to trace my neck. Groaning in desire, I threw my arms around his neck, heat flooding my body when he pulled me tighter.

"Dane . . ." I whispered, relishing the sound on my lips. He responded by pulling me into him even more, wrapping his arms around my waist and crushing my body against him. Even through the silk of my dress, I could feel the warm heat of his skin with the light dusting of dark hairs on his stomach prickling against my body. I gave in to my desire, pulling myself up higher and lifting my leg to put my left knee on the countertop, letting me kiss him more easily.

Dane's right hand let go of my back to cup my leg, his work-roughened hand sliding from my knee to the hem of my dress before stopping. He was strong, but still almost gentlemanly as his thumb pushed the hemline of my dress up until his hand found the silk of my bikini briefs. He stopped kissing to smile at me in joy. "You're so smooth."

The gleeful, slightly dangerous glint in his eyes made my knees even weaker than they already were, and I nodded, enjoying the seduction game we were playing.

Dane licked his lips, lifting me up by the hand that was cupping my ass and spinning us both around. In an instant, he had me propped up on the countertop, his hands at the hem of my dress, lifting it up. He stopped when the hem bunched up against the marble, stepping back. "Wait."

"What?" I asked, my heart hammering and my chest heaving. My nipples ached inside my dress, and I was sure I was showing through. I could barely contain myself, and now he wanted to stop? Was he having some last second surge of timidity, or was some other reason stopping him? "What's wrong?"

"I . . . It's been a while for me," Dane admitted without a hint of shame. He said it matter-of-factly, as if he were saying the sun is hot, water is wet, or that he was sexy as hell. "I forgot that it's probably better to lift your hem up a bit before you sit down on the dress."

I laughed as I realized what he was talking about, even more enchanted and turned on by his honesty. "Well then," I said, sliding off the counter and taking the hem of my dress in hand, "there we go."

The look in Dane's eyes and the little twist of his lips set me on fire even more. The cut on his cheek had stopped bleeding, but it still added a rakish sexiness to his appearance, like he was carrying his battle scars and would keep them as a reminder of what he'd done to gain my attention. I was kind of glad I'd worn one of my sexier sets of lingerie that night, mostly because it fit well under my dress, but the nearly sheer bra cups and silk panties certainly had the right effect on Dane. Looking down, my throat went slightly dry looking at the bulge in his jeans. He wasn't wearing any sort of overly tight skinny jeans either. He had to be big. Blinking, I looked up at Dane and bit my lip. "Better?"

"Much," he said, his voice as hoarse as mine felt. Grabbing my hand, he pulled me into a warm and powerful embrace again, this time lifting me in his arms and carrying me to the bed in the back of the loft room. The bed was a queen size, but that was more than big enough for the two of us as we tumbled to the mattress.

His lips found mine once more, this time his tongue wrapping around mine as he pulled me on top of him, my legs automatically parting to each side of him. I gasped when my panties came into contact with the bulge in his jeans, which already felt hot and delicious. "Oh, God . . ."

Dane pulled back to look in my face, worried for an instant. It touched me that such a powerful man could be both demanding and respectful at the same time. He studied me for a second before grinning, reading my expression. "It's been a while for you too?"

I nodded, suddenly shy. "Sorry."

He shook his head, his hand coursing up and down my backbone. "Abs, there's no need to feel ashamed of that. I'm honored, actually."

Nobody had called me Abs before, not even my friends, and to hear the word on his lips sent ripples through me. I enjoyed the name and mouthed it silently as he kissed my throat and along my pulse line. Abs. It would be my special name from Dane, and one nobody else would ever use.

He stopped his hands on my bra strap, and without too much fumbling undid the clasp at the back. Bringing his hands around to my sides, he slid my bra off until the only thing keeping it on was that it was sandwiched between us. Grinning, he pushed me back and let it fall off, where I tossed it off the side of the bed. My breasts hung in front of him while I ground over the bulge in his jeans, and by the look in his eyes, I'd never felt more beautiful in my entire life.

Hot sparks shot through me when he cupped my breast and ran

his thumbs over my nipple. I couldn't resist, and I started riding his bulge in my panties, the friction mixing with the electricity in my breasts to render me senseless. The whole time, his eyes bored into mine, but this time the gray wasn't brooding or dark, but instead wise and comforting. They were eyes that captured my attention, along with the growing confident smile on his face. It may have been a long time for him, but like riding a bicycle, he quickly remembered exactly what he was doing.

When Dane pulled me down to him, replacing his hands with his mouth on my nipple, I whimpered. It felt so good. His tongue found all the little spots that left me mewling and gasping. My hips sped up, and I nearly cried out in frustration when he rolled me off him and turned both of us onto our sides. "Why'd you stop?" I whined, unable to help myself. "I was nearly there."

"And so was I," he said with a little laugh. "Don't worry, I'll take care of you."

It was something in the way he said it that opened up more than my libido and cracked through the defenses around my heart that every girl builds up. It was like he was saying not just that he'd take care of me sexually that night, but that somehow, without even knowing if I'd see him the next morning, he'd take care of me the rest of my life. All I could do was nod as he laid me on the bed and propped himself up on his left elbow.

"Now here's something I enjoy," he said, bringing his right hand down to the damp heat between my legs. His fingers were strong and confident as he rubbed me, my eyes fluttering closed because it felt so good.

I forced my eyes open to look into his, letting them drive a wedge into my mind as his fingers stroked magically. The silk of my panties aided his touch, adding just the right texture to his caress. When he brought a single finger up and across my clit, I cried out, unable to help it. My orgasm rolled through me, sorely missed. It'd been too long, even by my own hand, and never had anyone made me feel so good.

"This is the most beautiful thing I've ever seen in my life," he whispered softly as I clenched, my mouth open and my eyes staring into his. "I don't ever want it to end."

Neither did I. I'd never felt anything like it as the waves and warm pleasure rolled through me, my body fluttering under his fingers. I could have spent the rest of my life frozen in that moment. Still, the moment did eventually end, leaving me trembling and sweating as I collapsed back onto the bed. "That . . . that was amazing. Tell me you're not done."

"I hope not," he teased, his confident smile mixing with the tender look in his eyes. "On one condition."

"What's that?" a new, delicious tremble ran through me at the promise in his look.

Dane reached up to stroke my cheek, soft and comforting. "You take those off."

I shivered at the implication and nodded. "Deal. As long as you join me."

He blinked and looked down, realizing he was still in his jeans. I hooked my thumbs in the side bands of my panties, and I couldn't believe what I was doing. A quick hook-up or one-night stand wasn't my style. I wondered for a second if I was only doing this out of rebellion against my over-protective father, or if I was letting my guard down because he'd saved me. I pushed it away as soon as it entered my mind, returning to my anticipation of what was to come.

I rolled my now-wet panties down my hips, pausing just before I exposed myself while he finished his boots and socks. His eyes had never left me, drinking me in and making me feel wanted, beautiful, even a touch exotic. Standing up, he unbuttoned his jeans, holding the flaps closed with his right hand. "Together?"

"That's only fair," I said. "One . . . Two . . ."

"Three," Dane said, pushing his jeans down at the same time I pushed my panties all the way off. I had to pull my knees up to do it, which took my eyes off him for a moment, but when I saw him standing there, I was driven breathless.

If Dane had been handsome before with his shirt off, he was god-like nude. The light dusting of hair that I'd seen on his washboard stomach continued down. He had a fine amount of wiry black hair that extended down his hips and to his thighs, slightly curly and well-kept. It made him even more masculine, totally and incontrovertibly.

I glanced down and I shivered, this time with a touch of fear when I saw him. Dane, for his part, saw my trepidation. He looked at his cock and back up at me, understanding. "I'll be careful."

His words reassured me, and my knees parted without any difficulty when he climbed on the bed, his cock huge and pointing at my entrance. I was glad he'd brought me to an orgasm already. My body needed all the lubrication it could make to handle such a humongous man. Even still, he was tender and real, thrilling me with his gentleness.

"Please . . . just go slow?"

Dane smiled tenderly and nodded. He'd obviously had this sort of reaction before and knew what he was doing. "I promise, Abs. No pain, and I'll do my best to bring you pleasure."

I held my breath, certain he was going to spear me with his cock, but instead Dane leaned down and kissed me again, the softest and most tender kiss we'd yet shared. His hands stroked the hair out of my face as he held himself poised above me, just looking into my eyes and caressing me.

He reached over in the night stand to grab a condom, and I watched him as he slid it on. It only took a few seconds, but I was so full of desire that it seemed to take him an eternity.

Finally, he moved into me, and I felt the head of his cock start to spread me open. We looked in each other's eyes as he moved, slowly as he promised, rocking in and out so that the stretching feeling I felt melted into indescribable pleasure. He increased his depth in such tiny increments that it didn't even feel like he was going deeper with each thrust until I realized he was halfway inside me and still had more to go. Best of all, my body wanted more, and with all the desire built up in me, I knew I could accept everything he had. Smiling as I opened myself to him, we kissed again, this time more forcefully. I was pinned beneath him, his body holding me in position as he filled me. In one back stroke he paused, taking a deep breath. I nodded, knowing what was coming. "I can take it."

The next thrust seemed to stretch on forever, and nerves I'd never even known I had set into rapturous tremors. Dane didn't stop, though, with each thrust coming harder and faster. I didn't know how many times he stroked in and out. All I knew was that my body was alive in a way it had never been before. Pleasure and joy flooded every inch of me, from my toes all the way to the top of my head, and every time his hips slapped into mine, the level increased impossibly. Infinity squared, cubed upon itself as he filled me over and over, claiming me as his with not just his cock, but his eyes and his lips. I moaned his name in time with each of his thrusts, wanting not just sex but to give myself to this man, the greatest example of manhood I'd ever known in my twenty-two years on this planet.

How long we stayed there, my hands clutching at his back while he thrust into me over and over again, I'll never know. Time lost all meaning except in measurements of gasps, moans and heartbeats. I wasn't even sure if I'd survive; the intensity building within me felt so powerful. But I couldn't stop, and I begged for more even as my head tossed from side to side. "D—Dane!"

"Abs!" Dane growled deeply and protectively, his neck arching as he came. My body responded, clenching and exploding as well, both of us crying out as we came together. Blackness rushed up to greet me, and I embraced it, knowing that when I awoke, Dane would still be there, and I would still be safe and secure in his arms.

Chapter 4

Dane

After we'd fucked, both Abby and I passed out from exhaustion. I don't think it was long—maybe just ten or twenty minutes—but enough for our bodies to recuperate from the tremendous outpouring of energy we'd just had.

When I finally opened my eyes, I was sure I'd died and gone to heaven. Or maybe I was actually back in Leavenworth after getting hit on the head from behind and hallucinating. Then she sighed and turned in her sleep, and I knew it was real. Abby had turned into me, her head nestled on my bicep and against my chest, her left leg in between mine. I held her gently, afraid that if I did anything, she'd wake up and the fantasy of what I'd just been through would be broken. Instead, I thought about what we'd just done.

I hadn't been lying to her when I said it had been a long time for me. It had been over five years since I'd been with a woman. During my deployment to Iraq, I had the chance with a female aviation captain, but she was married, and despite the fact that she would have been willing to do just about anything, I didn't go there. I've done some terrible things, but relationships are sacrosanct for me. At the same time, while a couple of the guys I knew tried to get with some of the locals, I didn't want some poor Iraqi girl getting into trouble and possibly stoned to death because she and I had gotten frisky.

Then, of course, there was prison, which had plenty of its own challenges. There were ways to set it up if you really wanted some action, but it would cost you. I spent the entire time in prison with nothing but my hand to help me. Well, that, a decent memory, and a good imagination. In the three months since I'd gotten out, I thought about going out and cruising bars or clubs. There were plenty of clubs that I could walk in, practically snap my fingers, and walk out with my choice of girls for the night. But prison had changed me. I wasn't a player anymore. I was looking for something more.

"Face it, dumbass, you were looking for something like this," I whispered to myself, freezing when Abby stirred in my arms. I meant to *think* it, not actually *say* it.

"You're hardly a dumbass," she whispered, nuzzling up against my chest.

If I didn't feel like a dumbass before, I sure did now.

Abby laughed softly and scooted higher, kissing my chin. "That was the most amazing experience of my life."

I didn't really know what to say. I knew the dangers of what I was feeling, and I knew that there were plenty of dangers in leading Abby on. She was obviously a good girl, maybe even the type that would think she was in love afterward. In any case, I could tell from her clothes, her speech—everything—that she was from class. Hell, even her lingerie looked expensive, something far nicer than I'd ever taken off a woman before. She didn't seem the type to have casual sex and take off, so I wasn't sure how to react.

I decided to just play it safe. "Thank you. I seem to have worked up quite an appetite. Would you like something to eat?"

She smiled that angel's smile that was impossible to resist. "I could do with some food, but nothing too big."

I shook my head. "Honestly, all I've got that's quick is some Ritz and cheese. I hope you don't mind."

"Sounds delicious. Let me put some clothes on so I don't get crumbs stuck in areas I don't need crumbs, okay?"

"Deal," I replied. "I should too."

We continued to lie there in bed, arm in arm, until Abby grinned. "You're not getting up. I thought you were hungry."

I smiled back, realizing I'd been lost in thought and hadn't moved. "I don't want to let you go. I'm afraid if I do, you're going to disappear and this will have all been a dream."

"What if I promise I'm not going anywhere, at least until you get me some food? Or better yet, until I give you my phone number?"

While another time with Abby sounded amazing, I had a feeling that anything between us would be doomed from the start. A girl like her would take off running after she learned who I really was. Even still, I was willing to take a chance. "You want to go out on an actual date?" I asked, wondering if she meant that or simply a booty call. Honestly, I was down for either.

"I don't know how you go about things, but this is unusual for me. In fact, I rarely sleep with men in general, not until there's a relationship involved."

"Me either," I replied, cracking a smile. "In fact, I never sleep with men."

"You've got a sense of humor to go with the rest of that package? I'm definitely saying yes if you ask me out on a date."

"Good to know," I said. "But what about work or school?"

"Oh, I'm not working at the moment," Abby replied with a small shrug. "Just classes. That way I can catch up and finish quickly. I kind of lost a year right after high school."

"What happened?" I asked, thinking back to my post high school days. I'd done quite a bit of partying, some motorcycle riding, and had gotten myself into a bit of trouble before the Army became a way to start to get myself on the right path. Or at least I *thought* it would be.

She shifted in my arms, unconsciously putting the soft weight of her right breast in my hand, where I cupped it without thinking, not squeezing, but just marveling at the texture of her skin. It was flawless, soft and unbelievably silky. "Actually, I was sent to a finishing school, if you can believe it. My stepmother felt that it was important before I went off to college. I think at the time, she wanted to push me into a school like Vassar or maybe Ole Miss if I insisted on getting a real degree. You know, one of those schools where young girls are turned into attractive, pretty little arm ornaments for their husbands."

"Not your style, I take it," I chuckled. It was now confirmed. She came from money, but the fact that she had rebelled enough to pick her own university told me something, too. "What made you go to Georgia Tech?"

"It's close to home," she said, "and it's got one of the best hard science reputations in the South. Georgia Tech produces graduates that do things, not graduates that just talk about things. That's the sort of people I like. What about you? Where'd you go to college?"

I laughed. "I've got a BTM from HKU."

"A what?" she asked, twisting around to look at me again. My hand was temporarily upset with the now-missing weight of her breast until she was all the way turned over, pressing herself against me and making sure my chest was now ecstatic.

"Black Top Masters from Hard Knocks University," I expanded. "The only education I've gotten past high school was courtesy of the Army. I started college but left before I completed my degree. Financial issues mostly, though I did get in trouble too. I wasn't a very good student."

"You mentioned jump wings in the bathroom. How long were you in?" she asked, moving closer to me. We were both feeling it now, but were taking our time, exploring each other's mind as well as our bodies.

Still, there were so many ways to answer her question, and few that I was comfortable doing. "I enlisted when I was about twenty-one, a few years after I finished high school," I said instead. "After doing my training at Fort Benning, I was in the infantry for the rest of the time."

"Really? So you're a real soldier then, not one of those armchair paraders," Abby said in a way that told me she was impressed not so much that I had been a soldier, but that I was the sort of person who wasn't afraid of hard work. "You don't seem too banged up to me."

"Looks can be deceiving," I replied. "The top and bottom three molars on the right side of my mouth are artificial. I caught something to the jaw there one time, and they had to fix it all up for me. I was surprised the Army did a good job. Even if you took a good look inside, you wouldn't notice a difference."

"Not someone's rifle butt, I hope?"

I was impressed. This girl knew more than she let on. Either that, or she had a penchant for enjoying war movies. I hoped it was her intelligence, because I personally can't stand war movies. They gave me flashbacks. "No, not a rifle butt. Actually, it was a brick. They gave me a Purple Heart for that one. What about you? Why biology?"

Abby grew serious and looked up above my head. "My mom and my big sister were killed when I was little. Head-on collision with another driver. Mom was in her Honda that she liked for running us around town while the other driver was in one of those big Fords they used to make—the Expedition, I think? You know, the small tank they made for a while."

"Expedition, Excursion, Excalibur. I forget the exact name, but I know what you mean," I said, lowering my voice to a comforting level while she shared this painful memory. "They were pretty popular for quite a few years a while back. Was the guy drunk?"

She shook her head, tears coming to her eyes. "No, it was still early afternoon, and Mom was coming to pick me up from my Gymboree class. I took that while my sister took her piano lesson at the teacher's house two miles down the road. The driver was a diabetic who was trying to treat his disease through self-medication and trying one of those no-carb diets. He went into diabetic shock behind the wheel of his truck and drifted over into Mom's path. Even though they were both belted in, they hit each other going forty-five each. The crash . . . I don't remember the funerals, but the newspaper clippings Daddy kept said there wasn't much left. And all of it could have been avoided if the guy had known how to eat right for his diabetes. Later on, when I was in high school, Daddy had a small heart attack—too many Sunday breakfasts at Cracker Barrel. That made up my mind, and I decided to go into biology. Later on, I'm going to specialize in nutrition and really work to make sure things like what happened to me don't happen to anyone else."

We fell silent, this time a comfortable one. While my body was aware of the nude young woman in front of me, my immediate desire was not to have sex, but instead to protect her. I held her close and we lay there in silence for a moment.

I saw the glistening drop of the tear that was still on her cheek and wiped it away. "I know that was painful. But I'm glad you've used it to fuel your desire rather than dismiss it."

"You have to take the bad things that happen to you and turn them into good things," Abby replied. "That's what Daddy taught me during the years it was just the two of us. Sheesh, I must sound like a total daddy's girl, don't I?"

"You're not the worst I've heard," I said with a smile. "You should have known one of the girls that I went to high school with. Not only was she a daddy's girl, but she had her father wrapped around her little finger too. She was insufferable to deal with."

"Well, you won't have that problem with me," she laughed back. "We butt heads a lot. Still, he's my daddy. I know, I know, that is supposed to give me all sorts of strange complexes or mental problems, but I seem to be doing all right."

"I'll say." My stomach gurgled, and Abby looked down, patting lightly on my stomach. "I guess I really am hungry."

"So am I," she said. "Do you have something I can put on? I really don't feel like getting back in my dress already."

"I'm sure I can find something for you. You could just use a t-shirt of mine. I'm big enough that it might just drop past your hips."

Abby took my offerings and put them on. As she stood up, looking younger and cuter than ever, she started to laugh.

"What?"

"Nothing, it's just funny. We just met, and I'm already wearing your clothes." She laughed again, looking down at the massively oversized t-shirt and shorts. "By the time breakfast is over, I'm going to be claiming half the bathroom and putting my toothbrush in there."

When I didn't answer, she lowered her eyes, unconsciously crossing her foot behind her heel. I wondered if this was the pose and expression she took when her father chastised her. If so, I was surprised the man was able to deny her anything. She was so adorable. "Sorry. It was just a joke. I don't mean to sound like I'm already head over heels or anything."

I laughed. "Trust me, it's a tempting offer. But yeah, let's not get ahead of ourselves, or else your father might have a barrel for me. One belonging to a shotgun."

"I think Daddy would like you. You're the sort of guy that he likes, confident and real."

I wasn't so sure of that, but I wasn't going to tell Abby my misgivings as I went to the kitchen.

"You did save my life, after all. That has to count for something.

Dane, what exactly did you do in the military, anyway? Were you some kind of platoon leader?"

I chuckled, shaking my head. "With this ink? The commissioning boards would never even take a look at me. Besides, they like those with college educations to become officers. No, I was just your run of the mill, eleven bravo grunt."

I brought over the cheese and crackers. I'd found some grapes in the fridge and put them on the plate as well.

"I'm twenty-nine," I admitted. "I'd probably have been promoted, but I had a bad habit of not exactly following orders."

We kept chatting, and after we snacked a bit, we both drifted off to sleep, but when I woke up, she was standing at the foot of the bed. Her eyes were wide with shock and a slow-growing anger, a photograph in her hand. I knew the photo. It was from the side of the refrigerator, and one that I wanted to get rid of but never had. Chris had left it on the fridge from the old days, and I'd never hated it enough to actually take it down. Besides, it reminded me of how I'd screwed up my life.

For Abby, though, there was something different in her eyes. There was awareness, and a growing look of betrayal, which cut me to the bone. "How do you know Chris?" she asked, pointing at the photo. "Who the hell are you?"

## Chapter 5

## Abby

When I got in the shower, the warm water helped me wash away the exhaustion of the evening. My mind and my soul were refreshed, recharged, and ready for more. It'd been a long time since I'd gotten so little sleep, yet I wanted the time with Dane to never end.

It seemed that with every word we shared, every touch and every time our bodies came together, we grew a little closer. And the sex . . .

No man had ever given me the sensations he gave me, no man had ever been controlling, powerful and unrelenting, yet tender and comforting at the same time. It was as if every touch said, *I'm in control and you are powerless, but I will protect you and keep you safe.*

Washing my aching breasts and the tender areas between my legs, I smiled at the fresh memories. I'll be the first to admit that until that night, I'd led a pretty sheltered life, and I still believed that my little outburst against my father led to it all. If he'd just have allowed me to do what I wanted, I can't imagine ever going back to a stranger's place, no matter how drop-dead gorgeous he was. Even if he'd just saved my life.

My sex life thus far had been pretty vanilla—I'd never done some of the things that I'd read about in magazines or online. Even Shawnie, who was no party girl herself, described my sex life as boring. In fact, most often, sex for me had been lying there while the guy grunted and thrust for a little while before rolling off me and gasping for air. It was the epitome of a bad sitcom, and I was supposed to be in

61

the wildest days of my life.

But with Dane, we'd done things I'd only dreamed of. He tasted my body and ran his tongue along every erogenous spot I had. I knew from the first touch of his tongue between my legs that I wanted more, and that I'd never be the same again.

Still, even a long-repressed body eventually tires out, and it was time to wash up and go. Soon enough, the water finished sluicing the dried sweat and sticky residues of our repeated lovemaking from my body, and I felt as refreshed as I was going to get. I'd picked up my panties and bra from the floor of the bed area of the loft, tossing them in the washer on a gentle cycle. Now, after no heat tumble drying, they were probably the freshest thing I had to put on.

"This one goes out to all you girls having breakfast . . . in last night's dress," Katy Perry had said, and I smiled to myself thinking about it. Damn right. Fixing my left shoulder strap, I looked at myself in the mirror, thinking I wasn't looking all that bad. I looked more like a girl who'd overdressed for breakfast than a girl who was still dressed from the night before.

I finished teasing my hair with my fingers, wishing that Dane had an actual hair brush, or at least some sort of band I could use to pull my hair back into a ponytail.

I made my way out to the kitchen, and I could still hear Dane snoring softly. I looked around, knowing he must have coffee. I'd gotten into a habit of having a nice steaming mug every morning, and I simply could not function without it. I saw the coffee maker, and next to it a clear glass jar that obviously had ground coffee inside. I remembered Shawnie's admonition to me that coffee should be stored in a cool, dark, airtight place to preserve the most flavor, especially if it'd been already ground. "Shawnie would smack you upside the head for that."

Still, the aroma that came from the canister when I opened the seal was heavenly, and I quickly got a pot going. I preferred my coffee with milk or cream, so I turned to the fridge, reaching for the handle. I had the door halfway open when the photo held to the other side by a magnet caught my eye, and my hand froze. With trembling fingers, I took the magnet off the face in the photo it had been covering, my mouth going dry.

I hadn't seen or heard from Chris Lake in years—not since he had what he described as an "incident" in Iraq. I'd been in high school at the time, so proud to be dating a handsome guy like him. I was even more proud of the fact that he was a soldier, and at the time, I thought he was out there defending our country. His final letter to me was long, and I remembered it was somewhat rambling. He'd lost a friend, he said, and another went to jail for the killing. As I looked at the three faces in the photo—one was clearly Chris, the other clearly Dane, but there was another that I didn't know. Right then, fear stabbed icily into my heart.

Marching to the bed, I stood at the foot, not sure what to do or say. Fear kept grabbing at me as I saw the things that I dismissed earlier. The amateur nature of some of Dane's tattoos . . . they could have just been ones done hastily in the service, or could they have been prison ink? When he talked about his time in the military, he hadn't really said where he'd been or even why and how he'd gotten out. Had he been the man Chris had told me about? Had I spent the night making love to a murderer? It couldn't be. Dane seemed nothing like a killer . . .

Before I could say anything to wake him up, he stretched his arms to the sides and opened his eyes. He blinked a few times when he saw me, obviously confused by what I was doing standing there. "How do you know Chris? Who the hell are you?"

Dane's eyes flickered between the photograph and my face as anger and shame built within me. "Abby, I . . ." he said, his voice trailing off into silence. For the first time, I saw secrecy in his eyes, and shame of who he was and what he'd done. "This isn't my apartment."

"Well, that explains a few things," I said, trying not to sound snippy and vindictive. I've got a temper, and a very sharp tongue to go with it if I let it loose. "Anything else around here not yours?"

He sat up, pulling his knees to his chest and scooting back. It enraged me, seeing him trying to take a cute defensive body position when he was obviously more than he'd led me to believe. Or perhaps less, depending on how you looked at it. "Almost all of it," he sighed, looking around. "I'm house sitting for Chris while he took a couple of months in Europe. He wanted to catch a festival in Switzerland and the last of the spring skiing or something, he said. I didn't have anywhere to stay, so he was basically doing me a favor. I've been trying to find a job the whole time."

"Not too many people want to hire a murderer," I spat, my anger boiling over. Dane recoiled as if I'd slapped him across the face. Still, he didn't deny it, which for some reason made me even angrier. I guess I still had a semblance of hope that I was wrong. "So what were you doing last night, huh? Deciding to hang out with the other assholes and felons in the park? You all have some sort of convention or something?"

"Abs, I never hurt you," Dane said, trying to defend himself. "I would never hurt you. I'm not like that."

"No? Then what about the other guy in this photo? What's his name and where is he now?" I nearly screamed, almost throwing the picture in his face.

Dane hung his head, guilty. "Lloyd. Lloyd James, from Gettysburg, Pennsylvania."

The name clicked, and now I could place Dane's as well. "Yes . . . Lloyd James. You know, Dane, you're kind of famous in some circles. Killers and those who betray their comrades aren't too popular in places like Atlanta. Why the hell did you come here instead of someplace a little less military-friendly? You have a death wish or something?"

Dane shook his head. "Chris . . . Chris offered me a chance to start over. After the conviction, my family said they wanted nothing to do with me. My parents, even my brother and sister . . . nobody came to see me for the whole time I was in Leavenworth. Chris did, one time. He also wrote me a few times—nothing much, but he was the only one I could turn to. Abby, I'm not a good man, but I'm not an evil one either. I . . ."

"I don't want to hear it," I snapped, cutting him off. "I'm out of here."

I stormed my way to the entrance, where I found my high heels. Slipping them on, I heard Dane get out of bed behind me. "Abby, wait. There's more to the story than you know. Hear me out. No one else will."

"No, Dane," I said, my own tears finally threatening to spill over. "I never want to see you again. This was the worst mistake of my life."

"Abby!" Dane's words followed me into the hallway, even though he didn't. They tore at my heart, which silently acknowledged that I hurt so damn much at that moment because I was hoping this could be more than a one-night stand. I should've known better, and I was being that naive little girl who thought she was in love after a man had given her the fuck of her life.

When I got outside, the muggy early morning air smacked me in the face, and I retreated inside. I saw that the Tower had a concierge, and I turned to it. "Excuse me," I asked the woman at the front desk. "Can you call me a taxi?"

"Of course, Miss," the woman said. Taking my face and appearance into consideration, her eyes softened. "Is everything okay?"

"No," I said, trying not to sob. "I just made the worst mistake of my life. Everything is definitely not okay."

## Chapter 6

### Dane

I watched Abby go, fleeing into the empty elevator and the door closing behind her. I couldn't move, frozen in shock at what had happened in the last five minutes. Walking to the door, I stared at the elevator as the lights showed it going down all the way to the lobby. Part of me wanted to run after her, to charge down the fire escape stairs and plead for her to listen to me. If she just knew my story, if she only could understand, maybe there'd be a chance. But the other side of me, the side that had spent nearly five years in Fort Leavenworth as Prisoner Bell, stayed my feet. It was a good way to get myself arrested again, and from what Abby had told me about her father, a good way to fetch myself another felony, possibly even a sexual assault or rape charge. Two-time losers on a rape charge don't get much mercy from the State of Georgia, and the only way I'd see the free world again would be as a withered old man.

The cautious side of me won, which disgusted me even as I closed the door. Something rustled at my feet, and I looked down to see the photo that had set the whole thing off lying on the tile. Abby must have dropped it when she fled the apartment, perhaps when she was putting her shoes on. Reaching down with nearly numb fingers, I picked it up, absently locking the door behind me as I looked at the faces in the photo. Myself, Chris Lake, and Lloyd James. The killer, his friend, and the man who'd damned me.

\* \* \*

*Northwestern Iraq, Five Years Prior*

"Man, do you even know what the fuck the name of this shit hole is?"

I glanced over at Lloyd, who was staring through slitted eyes at the wind scoured vista before us. We were inside a small hut that the locals had abandoned with the amount of insurgent activity in the area. It was just before sunset, and I was trying to get some rest and food before going out on guard duty starting at seven. Three hours of guard duty followed by six hours of sleep. It wasn't that bad of a setup, as long as we didn't get hit by the insurgents. Then nobody would get any sleep.

"What a shit hole," Lloyd repeated, and I had to agree that our hut didn't give us anything to send home on a postcard. It wasn't that Iraq didn't have its fair share of beautiful scenery. In the two months that we'd been there, I'd seen plenty of breathtaking sunrises and sunsets, and there was an arid majesty to a lot of the country. But still, we were uninvited guests surrounded by a lot of people with a lot of guns who didn't exactly like us. It got to you after a while. And this particular little nameless village had the unfortunate luck of being not only partially destroyed by insurgents, but it was hosting me and my squad mates just as a dust storm started to roll in, turning the whole world a sickly, ugly shade of brown.

"Lloyd, you know what the difference between you and the battalion commander is?" I asked, trying to get him to stop staring out the window and just calm down. Lloyd was my friend, but once he got going like this, he'd keep ranting through most of the damn rest time. No thanks. I checked the dust port on my machine gun, making sure to spray a little bit of lubricant into the action. I was on the SAW this patrol, and those things had a nasty reputation of getting jammed in the dust and grit of the desert unless you oiled the hell out of them.

"What's that?" Lloyd replied. "He's taking two weeks' leave to be back fucking some *fraulein* in Baden-Baden or something?"

"Nope. You're sleeping in the shit hole here. He's sleeping in the one ten kilometers down the road," I said with a smile. "Come on, man. This has been an easy patrol. We're scheduled to rotate back to the Green Zone for some R and R soon anyway. Just chill the fuck out and we'll be eating steaks, watching the NBA playoffs, and maybe getting some Air Force pussy before you know it."

"Forget that, man. I'm looking for a little local action," Lloyd said. "You know those girls want it. They dream about fucking a good ol' American soldier. At least I can take some good memories back from this dreadful place."

The flap to the room we were in opened before I could reply, and Chris Lake, our team leader and good friend, walked in. "Lloyd, careful what you say," he cautioned his buddy. "You know if the El Tee or the Captain hear you talking like that, you're going to be humping nothing but a rucksack for the next ten months."

I nodded. Lloyd had, in the two years I'd known him, slept his way through just about every town we'd come to. He had the looks for it, certainly. A bit shorter than me at just under six feet, with blond hair and blue eyes, he looked like Captain Fucking America, especially with his shaved side crewcut. The All-American Boy, with All-American dick, according to him. Of course, Lloyd wasn't too choosy either, willing to shag just about anything tossed his way. We still kidded him about the woman in New Mexico who'd turned out to be a grandma.

"Fuck that, Chris. You know, not all of us have Miss Teen USA waiting back at home for us to come back and legally deflower the tender petals of her maidenhood," Lloyd replied, turning away from the window and sitting down on the dirt floor of the hut. It wasn't a bed at the Radisson, but it was a lot better than sleeping outside or in our vehicles. "Some of us have to make do with what's available, and I'm not talking about Bane over there with his right hand."

"Sometimes I use my left," I taunted back. I always did. I hated when Lloyd called me Bane. Just because I'm taller and pretty strong does not make me a comic book villain. "Feels like a total stranger. I just close my eyes and pretend it's your mama."

We all laughed at the tired old joke with the familiarity of old comrades. I'd met Lloyd during Basic Training at Ft. Benning, while Chris had come along a few months later when all three of us ended up going to Airborne School together. When we ended up all getting posted to the same unit, Chris had a chat with his company commander, and Lloyd and I were assigned to his team. We'd bonded well, and while there were perhaps a few teams that were more professional than we were, even our platoon leader, Lieutenant Locker, had to admit that we were effective. Part of it was our team spirit and friendship, which allowed our little fire team to perform nearly as effectively as a full squad. If I had to do a house-to-house sweep, I'd rather have Chris and Lloyd on my side than an entire platoon of Delta Force.

"That reminds me. Chris, you heard from the beauty queen recently?" I asked him. He'd met her during a three-week-long leave period back home, but I didn't even know the girl's name. Wisely, he'd never shown any of us a picture of her, as even the more polite troopers would have given him a lot of hell if the girl was even half as hot as he described her. "You know, something probably involving puppies, candy canes and sweet innocence? Maybe a little poem decorated with hearts?"

Chris laughed and shook his head. "No, nothing like that. I tell you what, though, boys. When we rotate back out of this sandbox, I've got the world's greatest gift waiting for me back home."

"Is it serious?" I asked, surprised. All three of us weren't too fond of commitments, after all. Chris usually chased high-end or different girls, while Lloyd was a very catch-as-catch-can type. Me? Well, I was actually the nice one of our group, believe it or not. I didn't go out looking to break hearts, though I'd done my fair share. Things never worked out, and it just sort of happened that we'd break up, sometimes with bad feelings, sometimes not. For Chris to be in love, it would be like finding out George Bush and Barack Obama were best buddies who played cards together. "Sorry. I just didn't think it'd happen so soon."

"Fuck no, dumb shit," Chris said with a laugh and a snort. "But what I do love is the idea of taking that sweet, sweet cherry and wearing her out. She's already said she loves me and is saving herself for me."

"You actually believe that shit?" Lloyd asked with a guffaw. "You don't think she's just telling you that while shagging every swinging dick back in . . . where is it again?"

"She's an Atlanta girl, just like me," Chris said, before realizing

71

the double meaning of his words. I had to give a snort of my own. "You know what I mean. Not a fucking word, guys."

I laughed, leaning back against the rough walls of our hut. Atlanta girl. "You said it, not me."

\* \* \*

*Baghdad, Iraq, The Green Zone, 2 weeks later*

Sure, Baghdad wasn't like going on real leave. Even within the city, years after we'd taken over, things weren't exactly making Baghdad a resort town or anything. Still, within the Green Zone, we could do things that soldiers liked to do, namely chill out, get some beers, and if you were really lucky, find a hot chick to share your rack with.

It was the third night of our time in the GZ, and for me, I was feeling pretty damn good. I was still bedmate-less, but there was a cute little supply clerk from the Indiana National Guard that had her eyes on me, and best of all, both of us were open about the fact there would be no relationship situations involved. It was pure sex, a little fun, and then we went our separate ways. I would have been able to seal the deal, too, if it hadn't been that I was supposed to pull guard duty that night. Guard duty in the GZ is nothing compared to pulling a guard shift out in most of the rest of the country. Between the hours of eight PM and midnight, I only managed to get two hours of sleep, and I drooped over my rifle while my Iraqi Army post-mate manned the tower.

It was just after midnight when I came down from the tower I'd been assigned to, and I was ready to head back to my bunk. Duty within the GZ was on a rotating basis, and I didn't need to wake up for

any formations or any of that other bullshit the next day, so I was
planning on trying to catch up on some sorely missed shut-eye before
me and Miss Gina Redman of Terre Haute, Indiana found an empty
building to occupy together.

I almost ignored the sound I heard coming from behind the
supply shed. It was a common place for people with uptight tent mates
or commanders with a bug up their ass to go hook up. While I
personally found no fun with the concept of rushed sex in the dark
behind a musty tent while sand stuck to the sweat on your ass . . .
different strokes for different folks, if you know what I mean.

I almost kept going back to my bunk when I heard the
whimpered cry from the girl, and the heavily accented words, strangled
with effort. "No . . . no . . . please . . ."

I have no problems with being in control with a woman, and I've
had chicks that liked it rough. But there's playacting and then there's
real resistance. I don't go for that. Darting around the side of the tent,
I saw a man pulling at the belt of his ACUs, holding what looked like a
local girl by the throat with his free hand. He had clamped down more
with his hand after her cry, cutting off all of her air. She was scratching
and clawing, but he was short and stocky, with the sort of arms that
came from lots of hard work and just natural freaky strength. Her eyes
were fluttering shut and her hands didn't beat quite so hard as the
blood flow to her brain shut down.

I didn't even pause, even though I couldn't see the man's face.
Taking my M-4, I jabbed the butt stock forward. It hit the man in the
back of the shoulder, distracting him enough for him to drop the girl,
where she fell to the ground retching and coughing.

The man turned around, and I saw in the dim light something that made my heart sink. "Lloyd? What the fuck are you doing, man?"

"What's it look like? I'm getting some sandy pussy," he slurred. He was drunk, and Lloyd was the sort of guy who could handle his alcohol pretty damned impressively. I'd once watched him down an entire pitcher of beer in ten minutes, get up off his barstool, and then throw two dead center darts on the electronic board we were playing on. For him to be slurring his words meant he had either downed enough to kill a small elephant, or he'd been hitting something a lot harder than beer. From the smell of his breath, I suspected the latter. It took a lot, but when he was drunk like this, he was nasty. "What the fuck you want?"

"You can't do this, man! You really want to go down on a rape charge?"

Lloyd reached to his right hip, where I saw the bayonet in its scabbard. We didn't use them often. In fact, our normal rifles didn't even have a lug to connect it with, but you could still find one if you needed it. "I'll finish her off. There won't be no rape charge. There's just gonna be another sad terrorist beheading." He grinned and turned back to the girl. "Now go the fuck on, Boy Scout. Let the real men handle this."

He bent down to grab the girl by her torn and dirty clothes, pulling the bayonet from his scabbard while he did. She wasn't very old, considering she was wearing semi-western style clothing and didn't have even a head scarf on. Our cultural briefings had told us girls who dressed like that were either part of Iraq's tiny Christian minority or underage. I couldn't let it go on.

Reaching down, I grabbed Lloyd by his arm and yanked him away from the girl. "Lloyd, no! Look at her! She's probably not even eighteen, for fuck's sake! Let her go, or I'm dragging you down to the MPs."

"Fucking bastard!" Lloyd yelled, pushing back into me. He knocked me off balance, the two of us tangling up and tripping. I knew Lloyd was strong, but when he landed on top of me, there was also anger and drunken rage in his eyes. My right arm was trapped, sandwiched between him, my M-4 and my body, while my left arm tried to hold onto his right wrist. Unfortunately for me, Lloyd had leverage, and in his drunken anger, I thought he was willing to kill me. I'd seen that look in his eyes before, when he would be out on patrol and an insurgent sniper would take a shot at us or an IED would go off. His humanity dropped away, and a stone-cold killer would be there in his place.

"Lloyd, don't do it!" I yelled, trying with all my might to deflect or stop the slowly descending blade of the bayonet. But in the way we'd fallen, my legs were pinned, and Lloyd was able to put most of his upper body weight behind the bayonet. "Lloyd! LLOYD!"

There was nothing else I could do. I could feel the trigger of my rifle still in the painfully twisted grip of my right hand. I pulled, hoping that the barrel would wound or scare him enough that I could get his ass off me.

I hadn't realized that when we fell, the selector switch on my rifle had gotten caught in my web gear. The switch wasn't on single shot any longer. Instead, a long, rattling sound came from between our bodies, a sound that of all things reminded me of a beer belch.

Lloyd stiffened, his arm dropping, the point of the bayonet burying itself into the sand less than an inch from my left ear. He rolled off me, his body already going limp and his blood soaking into my clothing. I rolled with him, dropping my now empty M-4, amazed I was still alive and unharmed. "Lloyd? Lloyd!"

I looked around, hearing people coming our way. I grabbed the emergency compression bandage from the shoulder strap of my web gear, tearing the plastic envelope open. "MEDIC!"

\* \* \*

*Two Months Later- Fort Campbell, Kentucky*

"Specialist Dane Bell, you have been charged with the involuntary homicide of Specialist Lloyd James. How do you plead?"

I looked at my JAG lawyer, who nodded in encouragement. He was a wimp, the kind of officer who would have gotten himself shot if he'd been in any combat unit, and I felt an inherent sort of disgust for him. I'm not one of those types that cannot appreciate any soldier but those who sling a rifle, but my lawyer wasn't a man, in the real sense of the word. He was a weasel. I felt I was getting screwed royally, but by the way he put it, the odds were against me if I didn't do it his way. Without him helping in my defense, the odds were impossibly against me. "Guilty, sir."

The judge, a grizzled, hawk-faced Colonel who probably had done push ups with Patton and ruck-marched with Chesty Puller, glowered at me from the bench. I could understand. I'd just admitted to killing not only another soldier, but my friend as well. A Court Martial is not the sort of place where soldiers are given a pat on the back and toasted with beer.

Unfortunately for me, there were a few problems with my case. First of all, the Iraqi girl that Lloyd had been choking turned out to be the little sister of one of the local insurgency leaders in Baghdad. So, despite her repeated assertions to the Baghdad police that I had saved her life, her story was dismissed as being nothing more than the lies of a terrorist sympathizer. That she was underage and had somehow gotten inside an American base in the Green Zone didn't help. I suspected Lloyd had snuck her in, maybe with the threat of violence, but I didn't know. Hell, she could have been scouting for a terrorist attack. I couldn't have been sure, but it didn't matter to me. Shooting an insurgent is different from raping a child.

Another problem was that a post-mortem toxicology report showed that Lloyd's blood alcohol content was nearly zero. According to what my lawyer told me, Lloyd at the time of his death had the equivalent of one beer in his body, nothing more. This, more than anything else, confused the hell out of me. I'd heard his slurring words and had smelled something stronger than beer on his breath. I couldn't figure it out.

Third, and perhaps most damaging to me, was the fact that my lawyer was not one of those types who was passionate about defending his clients. In fact, he'd have much rather been out of the service altogether, working admiralty law with his father up in Seattle. He'd told me as much himself at our first meeting. I wasn't going to get a passionate advocate on my side. So, when the prosecutor tossed me a bone and agreed to a plea-bargain for involuntary manslaughter, I took it. If anything, I felt I had to do *some* penance for taking my friend's life.

"Specialist Bell, the court accepts your plea of guilty to the charge of involuntary manslaughter. I've looked over the terms of the agreement worked out between you and the prosecution, and while I find them rather lenient, they are within the guidelines of the UCMJ. In addition, the court takes into consideration the statements of character from your team leader, as well as your service record, which until now, while not spotless, showed that you have served well. Therefore, the court will agree with the recommendation from the prosecution. You are to serve three to five years at the military prison in Fort Leavenworth, Kansas."

There was an outraged cry from behind me, and I turned my head to watch as Mr. James, Lloyd's father and one of the biggest businessmen in that part of Pennsylvania, exploded to his feet. "The hell you will! That son of a bitch murdered my only son! And he gets three to five? Are you out of your fucking mind?"

The Colonel glared at Mr. James and banged his gavel on the desk. "Mr. James, it is only at the request of the senior Senator from your home state that I have agreed to allow you to attend these proceedings. He is a personal friend of mine, and he assured me that you would conduct yourself in a reasonable and dignified manner. If you cannot, I will have you removed from the courtroom, and neither of us wants that."

Mr. James was red-faced, staring daggers at the Colonel before turning his attention to me. "I swear, you bastard, you will serve every day of that. And may God alone help you when you get out."

He sat down before the MPs could take him away or the Colonel could order him out, and I turned my attention back to the Colonel. When he was certain there would be no more outbursts from the gallery—other than Lloyd's father, the only other person there was a reporter from the Fort Campbell Public Affairs Office, who would handle the press release, military level newspaper story, and statements to the civilian press—he continued. "The court's decision is made. In addition, effective immediately, you will be reduced in rank to that of Private, and upon completion of your sentence, you will receive a Dishonorable Discharge, forfeiting all pay and benefits accrued during your time in service. Do you have any questions?"

"May I make a statement, sir?" I asked. Other than entering my plea, it was the first time I'd said anything, and this was the third day I'd been in the courtroom. In combat, military justice is swift and certain. In the rear areas, though, justice was less swift but no less certain. The Colonel nodded, and I cleared my throat, squaring my shoulders and standing tall. I may not have been accepted by the military any longer, but I still had my pride. "I . . . I'm sorry for Lloyd's death. He was my friend, and I wish he could have been here today. But despite my fate, which I will not appeal, I feel I have served as honorably as I could have done, and I have never betrayed my oath to protect our nation and our Constitution. That's all."

The Colonel nodded, with perhaps a hint of compassion in his face after my statement, then turned to two MPs who were acting as bailiffs. He'd read all the same evidence I had, and he knew that if I'd insisted on taking it to a jury trial, a good lawyer had a chance of getting me off. "Secure the prisoner for transport. This court-martial is adjourned."

## Chapter 7

### Abby

The house was quiet when I got back, and I was worried that Daddy may have gone to work. Brittany didn't work. I don't think she'd ever had a job in her life, and I could not have faced dealing with her alone. Not on top of all that had happened to me in the past twelve hours. But Daddy . . . I needed him, regardless of how childish it made me feel to admit it.

On the cab ride from Midtown back to our house, I kept turning over in my mind how damn stupid I'd been. It had taken me a while after I saw Chris's face to make the connection, but once I had, the name *Dane Bell* stuck out like a sore thumb in my mind. I had been just about to turn eighteen when I read the news about a soldier in the 101st Airborne killing one of his own in Iraq. Chris hadn't told me a lot of personal details about his friends at Fort Campbell, probably because of operational security, but the names Dane and Lloyd stuck out because they were so close.

I'd known that Chris was older than me when we first met, but it was charming that he was willing to wait. We'd met on a day that Daddy had let me come to the job site, where he was working on a new building for Lake Chevy. Chris had been there on leave from the Army, visiting his dad, and the two of us hit it off. Within two weeks, we were seriously dating, Daddy at first concerned about our age difference, but accepting it because he felt Chris was so mature and noble.

I, of course, felt the same way, especially when he swore his loyalty to me. "Honey girl," he told me when he had a three-day weekend to spend down in Atlanta before shipping out to Iraq, "you just happen to be the most beautiful thing I've seen in my entire life. Only a damn fool wouldn't be willing to wait for you."

We'd kissed. We had done a lot of that back then, and I'd let him get to second base. But the one time he'd tried to push for more, I told him no, not until I was done with high school. He'd agreed easily enough, and other than a hand on my backside when we would kiss in his car or out on the lake when we went swimming, he never strayed out-of-bounds again.

After the killing, Dane's name had been all over the news for a few days. Even though I don't watch a lot of TV news, Daddy loves his *Fox & Friends*, along with Hannity, O'Reilly, and the others on that channel. It had made for good TV at the time, especially when it came to light that Dane was from a so-called blue state and had actually left college to enlist. Normally, this would have been a cause for celebration, but for the fact that Dane had been involved in what the campus termed 'multi-faith support group,' and the talking heads termed an Islamic acceptance front. Also, the classmates who came forward to get their fifteen minutes of fame described Dane as a misfit, who'd partied and goofed off more than studied, so he had lost his scholarship. "So you see, this little liberal, guilt-ridden sympathizer decided that it would be fun to go and play soldier," one of the commentators had declared one night, the same day I'd gotten the email from Chris telling me about the arrest, "but when the chance came for him to show his true colors, he chose the enemy over his own friend."

That Lloyd's father had made the rounds of the talk shows after that didn't help matters either. He was mad as hell and used every chance he got to try and push for Dane to get more time. Listening to his side of the story, you'd think Dane had gone hunting Lloyd purposefully.

By that time, though, I'd been caught up in my own drama, too much to know the truth from the spin. Chris had written me an *it's not you, it's me* letter, leaving me eighteen, not knowing which college I'd go to, and having to go with Pete Stantz, of all people, to the senior prom since every other guy worth going with already had a date by then. I'd been considering Georgia Tech and the University of Kentucky at the time, but Chris's breakup made my decision clear. As time had gone on, the hurt healed, and until the night before, I thought I was pretty well off, all things considered. I had decent grades, Daddy was in good health, and I was happy.

At least I thought I was, until I saw Chris's photo and it all came rushing back to me. The hurt, the pain, all of it. Add to it that Dane had been amazing in bed, so wonderful that my body still yearned for his touch even after knowing what kind of murdering bastard he was, and I didn't know what to do except feel miserable.

The sound of the front door closing echoed through the house louder than I thought it would, only to be followed by the sound of footsteps rushing to the front door. I stood there, unsure of myself when Daddy came around the corner from the kitchen, his face lined with worry.

"Abigail Melissa Rawlings, where have you been?" he demanded, anger on his face until he saw the way I looked. His eyes immediately softened, and he stopped, holding his arms out to me. "Oh, baby girl, come here."

He hadn't called me his baby girl in years, not since I got over wearing my hair in pigtails back in fourth grade, but it didn't matter. I rushed over to him, burying my face in the cotton of the polo shirt that he normally wore to the office. Inhaling the comforting scent, I started to bawl my eyes out. I heard footsteps again, this time lighter and more measured, and I knew that Brittany had joined us. It didn't matter as I continued to bawl, tears and everything else pouring out of me as he held me tight, whispering comforting words that had little meaning except that I was safe into my hair.

"I'm so sorry, Daddy."

"Shh, we'll talk about it later," he said, in that way that told me everything would be all right. "We've just been worried sick about you, honey. Come on, let's get you up to your room where you can change clothes. Do you need anything?"

"I just want to sleep," I said, my exhaustion hammering into me. Despite the cat naps I'd taken during the night with Dane, I was shattered and barely able to stay conscious. "Please, I just need sleep."

"Then let's get you to bed," he said. "We can talk after you wake up."

I felt like a zombie climbing up the stairs to my bedroom, Daddy and Brittany helping me the whole way. Daddy stopped at the door while Brittany followed me into the bedroom, helping me with my clothes. "I'm sorry I was so strict with you, Abby," Brittany said after the door closed and we were alone. "I didn't mean to make you run away."

"It's okay, Brittany," I said, too tired to say much more. "I just . . . I need to sleep."

"I understand, honey," she said, tucking me into bed. She sat down next to me, brushing the stray hairs out of my face. "I know that I come off as a bitch to you, Abby. I'm sorry about that. I never had a daughter of my own before. But I do love you, and I want to at least be your friend. I'll never try to replace your mother."

"Thank you," I whispered, my eyes drooping. "I know you care."

I didn't hear her answer as the black curtain of sleep started to fall over me and I descended into my dreams.

* * *

By the time I woke up, afternoon had come, as evidenced by the bright light that poured through the windows to the left of my bed. Atlanta's a warm city, even in winter, so my bedroom faced west to minimize the amount of sunlight that came through the glass during the day. With the way my bed was arranged, that put the main window off to my left.

I yawned, feeling myself remarkably refreshed and much better than the weepy, sobbing wreck that had been put to bed hours earlier. Stretching, I thought about the conversation that I would have to have with them, but I was more prepared for it than I had been that morning.

I looked down at myself, not realizing how much Brittany had helped me get changed. I was still wearing the same panties as the night before, but I had on one of my sleep t-shirts and a pair of my old cheerleading shorts that I still wore for sleep and exercise. I went over to my dresser and peeled my shorts off, changing into a pair of pink boy shorts that matched a t-shirt bra that I liked to wear around the house. There was no need to make Daddy feel embarrassed.

I looked at the panties in my hand, seeing a faint bit of dried mess from the night before, and sighed. I wasn't so much panicked anymore as I was ashamed. I'd acted like a total slut, practically jumping on Dane's cock as soon as it was out of his pants. A few tattoos, a little bit of a bad boy vibe to him, and I melted right into his hands . . .

*And the way those eyes looked at me when he touched me,* the voice in my head said in his defense. *Face it, you were falling for him.*

*I was, but that doesn't mean I need to keep it up,* I bitterly said to myself. I balled up the panties and threw them into the hamper. Much like the night before, I scored, this time two points.

I headed downstairs and found Daddy and Brittany in the living room. Daddy saw me first and turned off the television, which had been showing a Braves game. "Good to see you awake, sweetheart," he said, setting his remote aside and standing up. "How do you feel?"

"A lot better, thank you," I said. "And thank you, Brittany. I saw that you helped me change. Honestly, I don't remember much of that part."

"You were pretty exhausted, Abby. Come now, have a seat."

I rubbed my stomach, thinking. "What time is it?"

"Just after two, sweetie," Daddy said. "You look famished."

I shook my head. "No, Daddy. I think I can wait until dinner time. That is, if you guys don't mind eating a little earlier than normal?"

"I don't think that'll be a problem, dear, but how about a glass of milk at least?" Brittany asked. She stood up, then stopped. "Sorry. I've been thinking, and I feel like I owe you an apology. I feel like a lot of what caused last night are my suggestions to you."

I took a deep breath, having a seat on the couch. It had taken a lot for Brittany to say what she had to me in my room. It had been just the two of us. There hadn't been a need to show off to Daddy. Her words had come from the heart. "Brittany, I'll admit that there was a part of me that got up because of that. I had an overwhelming need to rebel. But that wasn't all of it."

I took a deep breath and looked at Daddy. "Part of it was you. I know you love me. And I know you want what's best for me. But Daddy, I can't keep living inside the bubble you've built for me. And as much as it may pain you, I'm not cut out for the world that Brittany is so familiar with."

His face pinched, and Brittany had a worried look, but both of them held a respectful silence as I continued. "I'm not cut out to be a debutante! Nor am I the type of girl who enjoys putting on a thousand-dollar dress to drive over to Camden in April to hobnob at the Carolina Cup only to have some frat boy from Duke end up puking all over it. I'm blue jeans and t-shirts, and during the summer, sometimes I like wearing Daisy Dukes and a blouse."

"Yes, much to my worry, honey," Daddy said. "Why do you want to live the way I had to? Dirt in my hands, the sun on my neck, and sometimes my father having to choose between paying the electric bill and paying for food. I just don't want you to live like that."

I smiled and came over, sitting in between them, taking both of their hands. "Daddy, that's not going to happen. Your hard work has put me through GT, even if you never give me another dime in your entire life. You've put a roof over my head, food in my belly, and most importantly, love in my heart. After Mom died, you worked hard, but you also loved me hard too. And Brittany, I have to say sorry too. I know you were trying to help me, and I'm not trying to demean who you are or where you come from, but it's just not me. I'm sorry if I couldn't appreciate what you were trying to do."

Daddy squeezed my hand and smiled. "It's hard to believe that my little girl's grown up so much. I guess part of me still thinks of you as the little girl who used to want to do coloring books and would mess around in the old workshop with me."

"Part of me still is. But I've grown up, too. I know part of me is still a bit jealous that I have to share my daddy with another woman, and again, I'm sorry for that, Brittany. I feel like I haven't always been fair to you about it."

Brittany smiled and squeezed my other hand. "Abby, I think you did more today than anything I've seen to show me that, while you may not exactly fit in with some of the country-club set, you've got more than enough moxie to be able to stand on your own two feet. I'll be honest, I don't think I could have done what you've done over the past few years when I was your age. And one other thing."

"What's that?" I asked, somewhat stunned by her words.

"I love you very much, dear."

I blinked, smiling as tears threatened my eyes again. "I don't say it enough, but I care for you too, Brittany. You've got some ideas that I may not agree with, but you love Daddy, and that's most important to me. And if you don't mind, I'll take some of that milk."

Brittany smiled and nodded. "How about we make it chocolate?"

\* \* \*

Despite the improvement in my relationship with Daddy and Brittany, life refused to get back to normal. I was glad that classes were nearly finished for the semester, because I was too caught up in my own drama to be able to focus on tests or papers or anything like that. Still, I had finals coming up in a month, and I knew that when those rolled around, either I had to get my act together, or else my GPA was going to drop. With grad school admissions coming up soon, I didn't want anything to put my chances of getting accepted in danger.

The problem was, I couldn't get Dane out of my head. When I woke up in the mornings, his name was on my lips more often than not, and I hated myself for it. How could I still be obsessed and thinking about this man who was a killer? Was I really that hard up for a relationship, or was there something wrong in my head? I thought about those sick, twisted women who would write convicted murderers in prison and supposedly fall in love with them. Was that what was happening to me?

*He said there was more to the story,* the little voice in my head would say whenever I thought about him. *He sounded so genuine when you were running out of the apartment.*

*An apartment that wasn't his,* I reminded the little voice. *An apartment that he was only crashing in because he was a convicted killer who didn't have a job, and probably didn't even have two dimes to rub together.*

*You mean like Daddy didn't have when he was growing up?* the voice asked again. *And just how did he turn out?*

"That's different," I muttered to myself.

"What'd you say?"

I started, looking up, and realized that Shawnie had spoken to me. We were sitting outside a pizza joint near the GT campus, where she'd invited me to grab some lunch with her before her afternoon lab class. "Sorry, Shawnie. Just talking to myself."

"You've been doing that a lot lately," she said, taking a sip from her Coke. "People are going to think you've gone crazy."

I shook my head, wondering just how close to the truth she was. I took a deep breath to force my mind off the subject and looked over at my friend. "They already know I'm crazy, Shawnie. About the only sane thing I do is hang out with you."

"My case in point," Shawnie said with a laugh. She was wearing her typical campus clothing, a pair of jeans and a Georgia Tech t-shirt, the G and the H poking out a lot farther than the center of the shirt. If I was to be accused of being curvy, Shawnie was nearly a cartoon caricature come to life. She took it all in stride though, and more than once had shut down a horn dog that tried to ease up on her with a lame 'hey, shawtie' come on. She liked her men intellectual and cultured, something that was pretty hard to find around campus. "Seriously, though, is everything okay? You've been off for the past few weeks."

"Yeah," I said, sighing. "Just . . . well, remember that night I said I was going to meet you at the art exhibit?"

"The one by the German? Yeah, I remember being pissed off at you, and even more when I found out that you were at the dinner for Greg DeKalb, of all people. But you told me you got hung up on some stuff. Why, what's up?"

"Well, I tried to walk to the gallery," I said, and Shawnie held up her hand, shocked.

"You did what? Abby, Atlanta might be safer than it was a few years ago, and this certainly isn't Freak Week, but are you out of your damn mind, girl? And you're a native of this area. What were you thinking?"

I smiled and took a sip of my own Coke, reaching for a slice of the medium pizza we were sharing. "Careful, Shawnie. Your Sandhills drawl comes through more when you get all worked up. But, as I was saying, I tried to walk. I ran into some trouble, and before you say anything, I know I was being stupid. But I got some help, and the guy who helped me . . . I'm just having problems getting him out of my head."

"Ooh, I see," Shawnie said. "Tell me, was he cute?"

"He was." I nodded. "A little different from the type I normally go for. Maybe that's the attraction."

"So why haven't I been introduced to him? Afraid I'll try and take him from you?"

I was about to answer when my phone buzzed. I picked it up off the table and grimaced when I saw the number. It was Dane, and while he wasn't exactly pestering me with phone calls, he had called me a few times in the three weeks since we'd spent that night together. I hoped he'd have given up, because every time he called, I was almost guaranteed to dream about him that night. I hit the red call rejection button and set my phone down. "Because sometimes guys aren't what they seem to be."

Shawnie looked at my phone, then up at me, and sat back, tenting her fingers under her chin in the way that told me she was being perceptive. For a girl who was in school for engineering, she had a deep psychological streak that could either be helpful or frustrating, depending on the situation. "Really? And without going into too many details, since I can tell you don't want me to know exactly who this mystery man is, what is it about him that has you so worked up?"

I sighed and shook my head, confused. "Shawnie, it's just that . . . I thought he was a good man. But, how can a good man have done terrible things? I mean, he's been in prison."

Shawnie tilted her head, smirked, and shrugged. "You mind if I tell you something?"

"You know you can say anything to me. You're my best friend."

"Abby, you come from upper crust society. Atlanta upper crust at that, which makes even Charleston look downright Hicksville. I'm from parts of South Carolina where a lot of the folks I graduated high school with, their greatest goal in life was to get a job at the DuPont factory down the road and buy themselves a new Chevy pickup. Guys I used to date, the pinnacle of their entire lives will be the two years they played varsity football for the local high school. I guess what I'm saying is, you grew up somewhat protected. Now, I'm not saying you're prejudiced, no more than I am, but you never faced the choices that some of the people I knew had to face."

"I know," I said, thinking of some of the discussions she and I had shared over the years we'd been friends. "It's kind of what makes you special. You're also one of the few people I know who doesn't try to kiss my butt or hold it against me that I am who I am."

"You can't help it, just like I can't help being fine as May wine," she said with a laugh. "But what I'm trying to say is, there are times when good people either just make stupid mistakes or are forced into bad situations. Did you know, my graduating class's salutatorian is doing ten years at the Broad River Correctional facility back home?"

"Really?" I said. While Shawnie had been more than willing to share her observations on things or offer up a bit of down home country advice, she'd never really talked about her growing up in South Carolina except as an illustration of another point. "What happened?"

"He had a cousin in the county over that got in trouble with the wrong type of people. He agreed to help his cousin out by making a run over to the Myrtle Beach area to pick up a package and bring it back. Now, you know, I know, and yes, even he knew that nobody forgives a multi-thousand-dollar debt for running down to the Beach to pick up some doughnuts and maybe some crab cakes. But, he decided the risk was worth it to help out his family. So he took his car down there and picked up the package. He probably would have gotten away with it, too, if there hadn't been a drunk driver on the road behind him on the way back. They ended up crashing, and the cops found sixty pounds of weed in the trunk of his car. He got tabbed on a Class E felony, and even though he was eighteen and it was the first time he'd done anything, the judge was one of those hard-ass types who looked at kids like him and threw the book at him. Maximum sentence, ten years at Broad River. If he gets time off for good behavior, and a little bit of luck, he might be out right around the time you and I start grad school."

I thought about it, then shook my head. "So you're saying the next time he calls, I should pick up?"

She might have had a point, but then again, we weren't talking about naively smuggling some drugs here. Dane took a man's life.

Shawnie shook her head and brushed a strand of hair out of her face. "What I'm saying is that you should think about it before hitting that red button so hard or so fast next time. Is there something you don't know about this guy? Is there more to the story than what you know already? And also, more than anything, is there a reason you're still thinking about him weeks after you met him for only one night? Oh, and one more thing."

"What's that?" I asked.

"Are you going to eat that last pepperoni?"

## Chapter 8

### Dane

I was sitting on the couch that separated the bedroom area of the loft from the living room area when I heard the doorknob rattle, and insane hope flared inside me. In the time since my night with Abby, life had become painful at best. Each day had started with rolling out of bed, a desultory shower, and then off to find a job. My list of rejections was now standing at two hundred and thirty, the latest being at a soul food restaurant on Peach Street that had five customers along with one of the dishwashers in the back having gang tattoos when I'd put in my application. However, one look at the box and the details of my conviction, and the manager hadn't even given me the respect of waiting until I was out the door to throw my application in the trash. Instead, she had balled up the paper in front of me and tossed it in the trash can by the door. "Boy, we don't need your kind around here," she'd told me. "Now get out, and I don't want you here as a customer either."

I'd tried again afterward to call Abby, but just like she'd done the other times I called, it went to her voicemail. I'd left her a message, then went on my walks again.

That morning, though, I woke up totally broken. Lying there in bed, staring at the ceiling, the thought of trying to get out of bed, shower, and go out job hunting again was too much. Even the thought of going downstairs to the library and grabbing yesterday's copy of the *Constitution-Journal* just felt like too much effort. Even the time I spent in Iraq wasn't so exhausting.

So that day, I lay in bed until nearly eleven o'clock before my bladder chased me out of bed. I'd always been a guy whose body seems to run by an internal clock that rarely varied. I sighed. I had exactly five dollars left on me and not a prospect in sight. Still, there was no way I could face going out there that day, not after two hundred and thirty rejections. And especially not after Abby.

So I crashed on the couch, foregoing a shower for the first time in over five years, the first time since Iraq. Instead, I lay on the couch, watching as people with even more fucked up lives than I had yelled at each other over paternity tests, who was sleeping with whom, and who was going to kick whose ass later on. It helped. No matter how fucked up your life gets, no matter how low down the ladder of life you felt you were, you can always turn on daytime TV and find someone who is worse off than you.

I was watching a DVR-delayed celebration of Drew Carey giving away a new car to some co-ed from Cal Poly San Luis Obispo when the door rattled, and I sat up. The slight hope I had was squashed a moment later when I saw Chris Lake walk in. I mentally kicked myself, considering the Mayfair Tower is one of those types of places where guests can't exactly walk in and out without a lock code or being buzzed in by the front desk. If it had been Abby, I would have gotten a call.

"Hey, big man," Chris said, looking fresh and happy. Then again, if I'd just spent weeks in Europe catching the last of the ski season in the Swiss Alps, I'd probably be feeling pretty good too. "Taking the day off?"

"Hey, Chris," I greeted him, admittedly sulking. When he gave me a look, I shook my head. "Sorry, I just thought you were someone else for some stupid damn reason."

"She must have really rocked your world." He laughed, dropping his backpack and putting his wheeled suitcase next to the fridge. "Or did your time in prison change your preferences?"

His joke was made with a lighthearted tone, but when I didn't respond, he sobered up, coming over and taking a seat in the chair that completed the rest of the living room ensemble. "I was just pulling your leg, man. Sorry, I guess I shouldn't joke about your time in prison."

I shook my head. "It's not that. Just . . . it's been harder than I thought it would be getting out. I just couldn't take it anymore today. That's why you found me this way."

He looked at me with an expression of mixed pity and commiseration that was somehow more painful than if he'd just looked at me in disgust. "You're still struggling on the work front?"

I nodded. "Yesterday was number two hundred and thirty. And not even a second interview. I was going to go down to the day labor office tomorrow. I'm down to my last five dollars. Which, by the way, I have to thank you for, and I promise you, I will repay you. You didn't need to leave me five hundred bucks."

"Five hundred bucks for two and a half months isn't a lot," Chris said. "Besides, it was the least I could do for you. You're my brother, man."

I sat up, my hands dangling between my knees. "You're the only friend I've got left, Chris. Thank you for giving me a lifeline."

97

Chris shook his head and sat up straight. "You can cut that shit right now. Everyone needs a second chance. That so far you haven't found that chance yet doesn't mean it isn't out there. So here's what we're going to do. You chill out a while, let me unpack, then go get yourself cleaned up. I can smell your funky ass from here."

I sniffed, and I had to admit he had a point. While I'd showered just the morning before, I'd done a lot of walking to quiet my inner demons, and that was pretty funky. "Okay, okay, a good scrub down with the Irish Spring wouldn't hurt things. I suppose you're going to want me to find my own place soon too, right?"

Chris laughed and shook his head. "You're welcome here for as long as you need it. If I need to bring a girl home, I'll give you a heads up. Worse comes to worse, we can do the old tie on the doorknob routine."

"Remember, I didn't finish college," I said. "That must have been your frat buddies."

Chris had gotten out of the service soon after he'd gotten back from his Iraq rotation, just as the Army was starting to draw down some. He'd gone on to college and graduated six months before I'd gotten out of Leavenworth, just in time to bury his father. Now he was twenty-nine like me, and was half owner of the second largest chain of car dealerships in Georgia, along with his uncle, his father's younger brother.

"Frats wouldn't have me," Chris said with a laugh, "probably because I ended up with enough ladies to start my own sorority. But seriously, though, let me unpack and you chill, then go get washed up. Then we'll get dressed and go out on the town, my treat. I'm sure there's some woman out there with your name on her lips, just waiting for you to give it to her."

The idea of cruising bars with Chris wasn't exactly appealing, but I couldn't exactly say no. I had no idea how to explain Abby to him, after all, and if I refused his offer, he'd want to know why. "All right, man, but don't be too mad if I don't exactly hit a home run tonight. All that time in the exclusive company of men does make your game weak as hell."

Chris laughed and got up out of the chair. "I doubt that, Dane my man. The biggest thing standing in your way is that you just have that damned inconvenient noble streak about you. And you always were pickier than you needed to be. Just remember, a pair of sevens beats a ten every day."

I snorted at the bad joke, causing Chris's smile to broaden. "Besides, we need to go out and celebrate."

"Celebrate what? You not breaking your leg in the Alps?"

"Fuck no. Your new job. Starting Monday, you're going to be the new shop assistant down at Lake Ford-Lincoln-Mercury. That is, unless you have another opportunity knocking."

I sat there, stunned. "Chris, you didn't need to do that. Really."

"It's not charity. Trust me on that. I may be half owner, but other than getting my Uncle Hank to agree to hire you, I've got very little to do on the day-to-day operations of that place. You're going to be working your ass off for your paycheck."

"And just what will you be doing?" I asked, feeling the first smile in a while creep out on my face. "Selling used F-150s?"

"No," Chris said with a laugh. "I've got my own job. Don't you know? You're looking at one of the managing partners in Lake-Crawford Real Estate. Starting tomorrow, I've got to start actually putting all that shit I learned in college to work. Use it or lose it, you know?"

* * *

Hank Lake was the epitome of a Southern good old boy. With sun-pinked skin and a slightly piggish look to his face, he could have done justice to a remake of *The Dukes of Hazzard* as a double for Boss Hogg. That being said, he was a lot gentler than his outer expression put off. In fact, he was a pretty good guy.

"Bell," Hank said one evening as I was sweeping up the mechanics' bay. It was one of the duties of my job, along with fetching tools, unloading and sorting parts deliveries, and a lot of go-fer work in general. I couldn't complain though. Chris had arranged that I was getting twelve bucks an hour, and each of the two weeks I'd been there so far, there'd been the chance to catch a few hours of overtime. "Come by my office when you're done with the bay."

"Yes sir, Mr. Lake," I said, putting my broom aside. I still had two more steps to clean the floor, since it was a Friday. After the initial sweep, I had to scatter absorbent material over any obvious oil spots, let it dry, and then sweep those up before mopping the whole bay with a strong detergent that was supposed to break up any thin layers of oil. If there were a lot of spots for the absorbent stuff, it could take upwards of an hour and a half to do the whole thing. Thankfully, that night there were only two, both of them small and in bay four, the left-most bay. By the time I finished the first three repair bays, I was able to sweep up the absorbent material, which now looked a lot like wet kitty litter, and get bay four done without too much delay.

I found Hank in his office, located inside the sales area. He wasn't a salesman. He'd let his brother deal with that side while he concerned himself with the mechanical side of things, but as the now operations owner of the whole chain—four dealerships throughout central and southern Georgia—he'd had to leave the greasy coveralls behind. In the little bit of time I'd worked there, it seemed to me that he wished he was back in the garages instead of wearing a white duck, cotton button-down shirt. I knocked on his door frame, a habit from my military days I hadn't yet lost. "Mr. Lake? I just finished bay four. Sorry if you were waiting."

He looked up from his desk, which was covered in paperwork and invoices, so much so I had no idea how he kept it organized. He must have had one hell of an assistant. "Not at all, Bell. Trust me, there's always more work to do with keeping this place going. Have a seat."

I looked down at my stained and spotted coveralls, and shook my head. "No offense, sir, but I'd mess up your office. If it's all the same to you, I'll stand."

Hank nodded, looking my clothes over. "Suit yourself. I just wanted to give you your first paycheck personally, so here you are." He handed over the envelope, which I glanced at before putting it in my back pocket. "You're not going to open it?"

"No, sir. I was taught that you don't tear open letters and stuff like that when the person giving it to you is still there. Either it's good news, in which case it can wait, or it's bad news, in which case you don't want to lose your temper in front of who gave you the letter.

101

Besides, I trust you, and I've kept track. To be honest with you, no matter what it is, it'll seem like a fortune."

Hank sat back in his chair, entwining his fingers over his belly. "I'm going to be honest with you, Bell. When my nephew said he wanted me to give you a job, I was confused. I don't know if you know, but he and that boy, Lloyd, knew each other before they enlisted in the Army."

I shook my head, surprised. "No, I didn't, sir. I always thought that the three of us met at Benning in Airborne School."

Hank chuckled. "Nope. That boy, Lloyd—his parents are from right here in Atlanta, same as Chris. In fact, Lloyd's daddy and I were high school classmates. Lloyd and his folks moved up to Pennsylvania right after he finished his junior year in high school. You never noticed he had an accent?"

"Lloyd was one of those guys whose accent never really gave him away," I said. "Maybe he blended his Southern with a bit of Yankee or something. Besides, a lot of us ended up with a bit of accent after a while. It kind of all blurs together when we're in green."

"I see. Well, anyway, those two boys grew up really thick, and I was glad when they met back up in the service. Guess what I'm saying is, if Chris stuck it out for you, there had to be a reason. So, I'm gonna make you an offer. Starting up soon, the shop has a summer surge of folks coming in. Lots of trade-ins and lots of repairs as folks want their cars tuned up for going out to the lake or going on summer vacation. We normally bring in a bunch of new folks around that time to do the lower level mechanical stuff—things like oil changes, tire rotations and changes, things like that. Pay's better. We pay each of them fifteen an hour, and those that have skills have a chance to become full-time mechanics if they know what they're doing. Tell me, do you have any real mechanical skills?"

I thought, then shrugged. "I learned how to do the basics on a Humvee, and back in my high school days I helped my dad with a rebuild of a small block Chevy engine for a '79 Camaro he was doing as a project. We finished just before I enlisted. Prior to that, I did basic stuff at a Jiffy Lube down the street from my house. But I never got any formal schooling or anything like that, if that's what you are asking."

Hank laughed. "I never went to any of those schools myself. I started the same way you did, rebuilding small block Fords with my daddy and doing oil changes here in the shop, back when this was a one-dealer operation. All right, then. The offer's on the table. You keep working hard as you've been the past two weeks, and tell me by the start of next month if you want a slot in the program or not. I'm not saying it'd be permanent. You might find yourself sweeping bay floors again come fall, but it'd be something."

"Thank you, sir. I'll think it over."

On the way back to the apartment, I did exactly that, mulling it over. Hank didn't strike me as the sort of man who would try and feed me a line of junk, so the offer did make me happy. I was a little disturbed by what I'd learned about Chris and Lloyd, but in the end, I figured that they'd just forgotten to mention it during the time we had been friends together. After all, military time was just different from civilian time. There's no other way to really put it. I didn't tell them too much about my life growing up in the Midwest, either.

When I got back, I found Chris leaning back on the sofa, watching the evening news. "Hey man, how was work today?"

"Good," I said with a smile. I pulled my paycheck, which I'd opened on the MARTA, out of my back pocket. "Check it out. After taxes, nine hundred and forty-seven dollars and thirty-six cents."

Chris flashed me a thumbs up. "That's good. You've been working your ass off. So are you on the schedule for tomorrow?"

I shook my head. "Nope. I'm off until Saturday morning. Why?"

"We're going out then," Chris said, getting off the sofa. "But you're buying the beer."

"I don't know, man. Since getting out, I've found that my taste for alcohol isn't what it used to be," I said, tilting my head and rubbing my hand through my hair. "You know, getting dried out by Leavenworth and everything. Not to mention, I don't need any trouble with John Law."

Chris wasn't to be denied, however. "Don't sweat it, man. We're just going out to celebrate. I promise, you're not going to get hammered, and we're just gonna relax, see if maybe we can find you a girl to take your mind off whoever the hell it is that's been keeping you tossing and turning on the sofa at night."

"Sorry about that," I apologized, knowing exactly what Chris was talking about. In the days since the night with Abby, she was always in my thoughts. A lot of it was silly shit, like if she'd be proud of me for how I worked or if she'd like the cut of beef I'd picked up at the grocery store. But whether it was just stupid rationalization or not, she was always on my mind. I tried to stop it, but the image of her eyes drove me from my sleep every morning, and it was the desire for my arms to hold her again that chased me in my dreams.

She'd even, after the week of sulking, fueled my renewed focus on working out. With Chris being home, I didn't feel so strange using the fitness center at the Tower, and I'd gotten back into the habit of morning PT. An hour on the weights alternated days with calisthenics and running around the park, using one of the jogging paths that ringed the place. Every time I went by the grove of trees where I'd rescued Abby from those scum that had assaulted her, I found the energy to push myself just a little harder.

Still, I woke up in the middle of the night more often than not, and I guess Chris had noticed. I made a firm decision. "All right, man. Let's go out and enjoy the world. We're single, under thirty, and we've got some money in our pocket. We're the kings of the goddamned world, aren't we?"

"That's the spirit. Come on. But first . . . you need a shower. You smell like a car service."

* * *

The club wasn't much, just a pretty standard country and western bar that catered to the crowd that was slightly older than college age. There were plenty of college kids there, but the majority of the people there that night at Roundups looked like they had at least a car loan, if not a mortgage, in their name.

Unfortunately, the fact that we were there on a Wednesday night of all times meant that the crowd was light. We'd been there an hour already, and to be honest, even if I had been in the mood to chase a skirt, the pickings were mighty slim, and Chris was despondent. "This place is dead, man. Sorry about that."

I took a sip of my beer, the second glass of the night—I'd promised myself no more than three— and sat back, shaking my head. "It ain't no thing. It's nice to just get out a bit and chill. Hell, it feels good just being able to pay for the beer."

"Well, you still owe me about fifty more pitchers, by my calculations," Chris said with a laugh. "Do that over the course of the rest of our lives, and I'll call it even on that loan. No way in hell am I taking half of your first paycheck."

"Dude, you need to at least let me give you something," I objected. "Pay you some rent, something. And we go half on the groceries."

Chris took another drink of his own beer—he was most of the way done with number four and warming up for number five—and it looked like he was about to object for a second, then he shrugged. "All right. We go half on the groceries, and your rent's four hundred a month. You pay me with your next paycheck."

Chris finished off his beer and looked around, seeing something that caught his eye. "Damn, check out the tits on that one. Phew, she'd be able to hold this whole glass in between those puppies."

I looked over and saw who he was talking about, a curvy girl who looked to be in her early twenties. She was pretty light skinned, but she still stood out in a place like Roundups, where most of the clientele was a shade lighter. "I see you still like chasing the younger ones," I said. "Though she isn't jailbait. When did you grow out of them?"

"About the time I started getting strange looks around the high schools," Chris said with another laugh. "So I graduated up to college girls, and that one looks like just about my type. You know what the best thing about undergrads is, Dane?"

"What's that?" I asked, feeling like the years were falling away. We weren't pushing thirty anymore but were twenty-three and on leave in between Airborne School and heading back to Fort Campbell to join the 101st, and everything was relaxed and cool.

"I keep getting older, they keep staying the same age," Chris finished with a laugh. "Why don't you try for that one? You always struck me as a tits man."

I shook my head. "Nah, that's okay." I looked around for someone else to take my attention from the girl, someone who looked like she was already attached. It wasn't that the girl wasn't hot, it was just I wasn't interested in a one-night stand. *Besides*, the inner voice said, *that isn't Abby.* "How about that one?"

Chris looked over at who I pointed out, laughing. "Her? Didn't think you chased married women."

I shrugged. "Maybe it's just the beer, then. Hey, what ever happened between you and that girl you were dating right before I went up? You know, the one we called Miss Teen USA?"

Chris polished off the rest of beer number four, his expression darkening. "Never came to anything, man. Just . . . never came to anything. Listen, you going to find some pussy or not? If not, I'm going to look around myself."

I looked around and shook my head. "Nah, I'm good. Probably got whiskey dick right now anyway."

Chris grunted and heaved himself out of his chair, putting his glass down on the table. I looked, and the girl he'd first shown interest in had seemingly disappeared, while the woman I'd indicated seemed like she was still there. Chris studied her for a second and shrugged. "Hell, any port in a goddamn storm. Yo, you good at getting home tonight by yourself if you need? I'd rather not bring this one home, if you know what I mean."

"I'm good, man. Happy hunting."

"You're goddamn right about that."

## Chapter 9

## Abby

I came out of the Clough Undergraduate Commons building, frustrated with myself. I'd stopped by the building to find a quiet spot to do some studying for my European History final, which was the next day, when I'd fallen asleep in one of the comfortable chairs that you could find in the study rooms. When a chime had woken me up, I was pissed to find that it was already noon, and I had agreed to meet Shawnie for lunch in fifteen minutes. If I hurried, I'd just make it.

Heading off campus, I rounded a corner to come to a screeching halt before I got run over by someone on a bicycle. "Hey, watch where you're going!"

The bike came to a stop, and I saw that the man was wearing a business suit, one of the seeming army of young executives on bikes that had sprung up around Atlanta as the city became more bike friendly. This one had the whole nine yards of gear, including aerodynamic minimalist helmet and even a protective tight spat on his right lower leg to protect his suit pants from the oil and dirt of his chain.

When he turned, I felt like I'd been smacked in the face. "C-Chris?"

Chris blinked, his momentary expression of anger over being yelled at being replaced by a gape of surprise. "Abby? Abby Rawlings?"

I smiled, stunned. "Yeah. Wow, it's been so long."

He got off his bike and came over, grinning. "Yeah, it has been.

How have you been?"

I shrugged. "Well, you know . . . nearly done with college now. And you?"

"Running back to the office," he said. "I had a client meeting downtown, and the traffic is hell in a car that way this time of day, so I jumped on the bike instead. I have to say, you look great. So you're what, a senior now?"

I nodded. He was the same as ever, with the sort of personality that never let up and never really backed down. "Yeah. What about you? What are you doing?"

"I'm in real estate. Hey, you know, we should catch up sometime. I live near here, if you don't know. The Mayfair Tower. You know it?" Chris said, smiling wider.

The mention of the Mayfair filled my heart with dread and trepidation as I thought again about Dane. It had been Dane who'd taken me to the tower, and it was through Dane that the memory of Chris was strong in my head again. Most of all, though, it was Dane. Dane, Dane, Dane damn-his-heart-for-disrupting-my-sleep-for-five-weeks-Bell. Chris saw the change of expression on my face and tilted his head to the side, confused. "Abby, I know that I was kind of an idiot in breaking things off between us the way I did, but that was a few years ago now. Listen, I'd really like the chance to at least explain to you why. Would you mind if I got your number?"

My cellphone buzzed in my pocket and I pulled it out, seeing that it was Shawnie. Cursing silently to myself, I nodded quickly. "Okay. Here," I said before giving him the number. I didn't have time to argue with him. I didn't want to keep Shawnie waiting any longer than I had to. "Chris, I'd love to chat more, but this is a friend of mine, and I'm already late for a lunch appointment. Do you mind if I take off?"

"No, I understand," he said with a somewhat happy smile. "It was good to see you again."

He hopped on his bike and disappeared down the street while I answered Shawnie's call. "Yeah, babe, it's me. Yeah, I know. Hey, I fell asleep in a study chair. You know, that one that gets the morning sunlight. I'm just off campus now, maybe five minutes away? Yeah, go ahead and order," I said as I jogged across the street. "General Tso's Chicken for me. I'm serious, and yes, I know it totally makes me a hypocrite. But today I can use it. I'll tell you all about it when I get there. Thanks, Shawnie. Bye."

I turned back to see if I could still see Chris, but he had disappeared. I was confused, and more than ever, unsure of what the hell was going on. Chris looked handsome, that was for sure, but there was something in the way he'd talked to me . . . I just wasn't attracted to him anymore. Sure, five years ago when I was seventeen, maybe. But not anymore.

When I got to the restaurant, Shawnie was just pulling apart her set of chopsticks. "Hey, Abby, the food should be here any minute. So how was your nap?"

"Needed," I said honestly. Shawnie gave me a look of concern, and I nodded. "Yeah, I'm still not sleeping well."

"Even after the double spin classes you tried this past week?" she asked. "You could barely make your way up the stairs the last time I saw you."

111

I nodded. While I'd pushed myself to my limits physically and dropped into bed each night exhausted, that didn't mean that I was staying asleep or sleeping well. "Not even those. Why do you think I'm trying the chicken today? My legs are so damn sore that I figure the extra calories and protein can do nothing but help with recovery, if nothing else. I'll be honest with you, Shawnie. I'm scared. Our history final is tomorrow, and right now I couldn't tell you the difference between Napoleon Bonaparte and Napoleon Dynamite."

"So when are you going to give this guy a call back then?" Shawnie asked, cutting to the root of the issue in her normal direct fashion. "At least talk to him over the phone and then make your decision. You might be able to get some sleep tonight."

"And tomorrow's final?" I asked, confused. "What am I supposed to do about that?"

Shawnie laughed and leaned back. Our food arrived, and we tore into it like the starving people we were. I hadn't told her, but between the stress, the extra exercise and the lack of good sleep, I'd dropped nearly eight pounds in the past two weeks, and even Brittany, who had once joked with me that there was a kernel of truth in the old saying you could never be too rich or too thin, looked at me with concern. I could see it too, as my cheekbones were starting to be a bit too defined, and I'd gone from perky and cute to lean and drawn. A few more weeks of this, and I'd be at the stringy and emaciated stage.

"I've been thinking," I told Shawnie after I'd finished chewing on one of the spicy-sweet chunks of chicken, "and I think what you told me last time carries a lot of merit. But, Shawnie, what if the thing this guy did . . . well, what if it's a lot more serious? That guy you knew in high school, that's one thing. But to do what this guy did . . . well, are there crimes beyond forgiveness?"

Shawnie chewed on some of her own food, Kung Pao shrimp and vegetables, then took a sip of her tea. The restaurant, in a nod to the Southern culture in which it was located, offered both iced and traditional hot tea with its meals, although they had so far not bowed to the Southern convention of adding ridiculous amounts of sugar to all tea.

"That's something I think each person needs to answer for themselves," she eventually replied. "I can't speak for you, Abby, but from what I've seen from you, I think you need to talk to him either way. Can I ask—you don't need to answer or anything, but from the way you acted afterward . . . I take it that it was more than just a kiss or something?"

"God, yes," I immediately said, blushing. "A lot more."

Shawnie nodded, then grinned. "It was that good, huh?"

I couldn't help it, I laughed. The humor helped. "You have no clue, Shawnie. Seriously, that man could do things that I never imagined."

"And your hang-up about him, is it because of that, or because of him?" she asked, springing her trap. It was part of the reason I liked her so much. She was willing to confront me, but always in a way that was for my own good. "I'm just saying, if you're having bad dreams and not sleeping because you need a good orgasm, I'll get you a battery-powered sleep aid for your graduation present. Rechargeable, even. But I think you're more authentic than that."

I couldn't help but laugh, and it gave me something to think

113

about. I took a sip of my tea, thinking. Shawnie and I worked our way through the rest of our meal when she took something out of her pocket. "Hey, I got a letter today."

"Oh?" I asked. "Who from?"

"Not who, but where," Shawnie said. "I got accepted for a full ride to Stanford for grad school."

I blinked, stunned. "Full ride? Really?"

Shawnie nodded, sighing. "Yeah. You remember that summer internship I did last summer, the one with the lab over in Texas?"

"Duh," I replied with a laugh. "Shawnie, you got to do a summer internship at the Johnson Space Center. What could be better for an engineering student?"

"Well, the guy I was working with there—I thought he was a total prick, but it turns out that he wrote a letter to the admissions people at Stanford. He's buddies with the head of the aeronautical engineering department there, and they've collaborated on some projects together. In any case, when my application went across his desk, the guy pushed for me. And by the conversation I had with the guy last night on the phone, if my first semester works out well, he'd be able to get me a paid TA position second-semester teaching freshman math too. It's not a lot, but it'd put cash in my pocket and totally eliminate the need for me to do a part-time job."

I whistled. "You must have really made an impression on the guy at Johnson."

"I guess I must have," Shawnie said with a chuckle. "I never would have thought it from the way he acted the whole time I was there."

"So what are you going to do?" I asked. "You know I've only applied to schools in the area. GT, Duke, UGA, stuff like that."

"I know," Shawnie said quietly. She looked at the letter, which she'd taken out of the envelope while we talked, then looked up at me. "Abby, you're my best friend, but this is too good to pass up. I mean, a paid Master's? Not too many girls from the Sandhills get a chance like that."

"Not to mention you'll be working with some of the best and brightest in the world, as well as being able to maybe score a job with the JPL, or maybe one of those aircraft manufacturers that you bent my ear about so much," I said. I reached across the table and took her hands. "If you want my advice, I want you to do it. I mean, of course I'll miss you, but we can still get together during summers, and besides, it'll give you motivation to make a plane fast enough that you and I can hang out on weekends or something."

Shawnie squeezed my fingers and lowered her head, blinking. "Thanks, Abby. I love you, girl."

"I love you too, sweetie," I replied. My phone rang, and I took it out of my pocket. I looked at it, then I looked up at Shawnie. "It's him."

"Who?" she asked, momentarily having a vacant moment.

"You know . . . Dane."

"Dane, so that's his name," she said while the phone rang. "So what are you going to do?"

I thought, my finger hovering between the green and red buttons. "Hell, you listened to my advice. I might as well follow yours," I said, jabbing the green button. "Hello?"

"Abby, it's Dane. Don't hang up."

I looked over at Shawnie, who gave me a supportive smile and sat back. "I won't hang up, Dane. But you need to talk fast, and talk well."

I heard Dane exhale on his end, and my heart went out to him. I'd been rejecting his calls for so long, he probably had little hope left that I'd have ever picked up. I wondered if his heart was in his throat like mine was, and if he was also torn in half between fear and happiness, although perhaps for different reasons.

"Abby, first of all, I want to apologize. You're right, there's a ton of things about my past that you don't know about. And maybe I should have told you. But I'll be honest in saying I just didn't know how. I need to see you. At least give me a chance to tell my side of the story. There's more to it than what you know. I'm not asking for redemption, but . . . I want to see if there is more between us than just one night. And most of all, I don't want you to think I'm a monster."

"Hold on," I said. I took the phone away from my ear and covered the mouthpiece. "He wants to meet. Not a date, just to talk."

"And what does your heart tell you?" Shawnie asked.

"To say yes," I replied. "But how should I set it up?"

"How about a coffee shop or someplace public? If you want, I can go with you."

I smiled in appreciation at her offer and nodded. Uncovering the mouthpiece, I took a deep breath. "All right, Dane, but it's where I want and on my terms, agreed?"

"Agreed," he said immediately, relief evident in his voice.

"Good. Then meet me at The Nook, on the edge of Piedmont

Park. You know where that is, I assume?"

"Just down the street," Dane said eagerly. "What time should I meet you there?"

"You can meet *us* there at seven thirty. But Dane, if we don't see you by seven thirty-five, I'm walking out and blocking your number. Okay?"

"I'll be there," he said. He was so eager, he didn't even ask who the other person was. "Abby?"

"Yes, Dane?"

"Thank you. I'll see you tonight."

"Good-bye, Dane."

I hung up my phone, looking over at Shawnie. "So, what do you say to the two of us getting one more study session in on European History before I take you out for burgers and tots at The Nook?"

Chapter 10

Dane

I was nervous standing outside the door to The Nook, even more nervous than at my court martial. The tavern wasn't too busy for a Tuesday night, but I'd still made sure to arrive five minutes early. I was wearing my best clothes short of a suit, which I still didn't own. Instead, I'd put on my best pressed-collared linen shirt, dark khaki dress pants, and my only set of dress shoes, slip-on black shoes that I'd polished not to a military-level shine, but still pretty good.

I looked down at myself and nearly slapped my head. I felt so stupid. The night I'd met Abby, I'd been wearing jeans and boots and a t-shirt underneath my hooded shirt. Now, I probably looked like a loser who was trying to look like something he wasn't. "The worst that can happen is she says no. You've gotten plenty of that in your life."

Somewhat reassured, I entered the place, looking around for

Abby's face. I panicked for a second after my first look didn't see anything, but then when I checked again, I saw what looked like a familiar face behind a burly-looking man at a corner table. She was seated with a friend, I guess, and I did a double take when I realized it was the same girl that Chris had his sights on back at Roundups.

I went over, her friend seeing me first. She leaned over, and Abby turned, finding me and raising her hand not so much in a wave as a signal that I had found the right table. I couldn't help it. My heart jumped in my chest when our eyes met, and it felt like at least a little bit of the weight that had been sitting on my shoulders since she'd run out of the apartment was gone.

"Abby . . ." I said, not sure how to continue when I reached the table. I wanted to pull her into my arms and kiss her again, to feel the lips that I'd dreamed about for weeks. I wanted to whisk her away to a fantasy land that didn't exist outside of movies. Finally, I knew I had to say something. "It's good to see you. Can I sit down?"

Abby's eyes cut over to her friend, whose lips twitched in an amused smile. "Sit down, Dane. By the way, I'm Shawnie, Abby's friend."

"It's good to meet you," I said, offering my hand. We shook, and I was impressed with her grip. Most women in the South either wilt or give you a weird sort of grip that doesn't quite align properly with the way a man grips your hand, web of thumb to web of thumb, fingers wrapped properly. Most women give you some sort of three-quarter grip where their thumb ends up right about the base knuckle of your fingers, a half-inch short, with their own fingers in some sort of strange stiff pincer grip. Shawnie could shake hands correctly, and I was pleased with that at least. "So I guess you're the other part of *us* that Abby mentioned earlier?"

"I am," she answered playfully. "I get to play the silent muscle, or the Inquisitor, whichever is needed. Do you have any sins to confess?"

Her eyes were twinkling in good humor and her mouth was quirked in a half-grin, but it faltered when she saw my face and reaction. "I have more sins than I can think of counting," I said somberly. "But I promise you both, I won't hide any of them."

Abby nodded, and for the first time since that one special night, I saw a faint ghost of her smile. "Be careful, Dane. If you think I'm the sort of person who asks hard questions, Shawnie's a pit bull. You may be asked things that you aren't comfortable answering."

"I know. I've been thinking about that for the past six hours. Hell, in reality, I've been thinking about that for the past month. And I'm willing to do that," I said. A waitress came by and took our drink orders—Cokes all around. "You're probably wondering why."

"The thought had crossed my mind," Abby said. "Shawnie's been asking me that too. Why would a man be willing to even try explaining things to a girl who he has known for only one night? Why not just find another girl, one who doesn't know and doesn't care about what you did?"

"I think it's because he's thinking with his hips and not with his head," Shawnie added with a wicked grin.

"If I just wanted to get my rocks off, there's a lot of places I could go. But I didn't, and other than two nights out, one at a place called Roundups with my friend, Chris, I haven't been in a night spot since Abby and I met. To tell you the truth, I've seen you before. You were there that night."

"Ah, *that* night," Shawnie replied, totally unfazed. Smart and collected. I liked this girl. She was a great friend for Abby. "Yeah, I went by there. What did you think?"

"Beer's a bit expensive, but the music is tolerable. But anyway, I'm doing this because I felt like maybe we had a connection. I could be wrong, but I'd like to find out."

Abby's eyes softened. My words had an impact on her. Still, there was a lot of hardness in her eyes. Our tension was broken, however, when Shawnie interrupted. "Whoo, you're either the most romantic man in the world or the smoothest talker. Hey, barkeep! I'm going to need a beer over here to put out these flames!"

"So why didn't you tell me?" Abby asked quietly after the beer arrived. I demurred, taking just a sip from the previously ordered Coke. I didn't need any alcohol in my system. "Why didn't you tell me about your past?"

"I didn't think it really mattered at the time. I didn't exactly expect that to happen, and well, after it did, I didn't really know if I should or how. I mean, was I supposed to say 'by the way, you just slept with an ex-con'? How would you have done it if our positions were reversed? I'd feel like I was in a Carly Rae Jepsen song or a bad Internet meme. I'm a convicted killer, so call me maybe?"

Shawnie nearly snorted beer from her nose, but Abby didn't flinch, studying me with those perceptive eyes of hers. Finally, she nodded, accepting the point. "I do suppose that's not the sort of thing you tell someone in that kind of situation. Would you have told me eventually?"

"I'd like to say yes, but hypotheticals have never been my strong point," I said. "I'll be honest. Not a day goes by that I'm not reminded of what I did, of what happened. There are times, though, that I'd like to move past it, to not wake up every morning with the thought that I'm going to spend the rest of my life with this weight around my neck."

"Tell us what happened, in your words," Shawnie said suddenly, very serious. "Abby showed me some of the old news clips about your conviction. They said you pleaded guilty after killing another soldier."

I nodded and told them my version of the events. "In the end, I pleaded guilty because I could have done something different," I said. "I could have knocked him out. I could have kicked him in the back of the leg or something, something to have let me be in control and not end up where we did. That, combined with the case and who I had as a lawyer, I decided the best thing to do was to plead guilty."

"And if you hadn't?" Abby asked, almost all of the hardness gone from her eyes. "If you'd taken it to the trial?"

"The prosecutor was asking for murder," I said. "Conviction would have been either twenty years and up, or death. Considering it was in a combat environment, I most likely would have gotten life or the death penalty."

"So why Atlanta?" Abby asked. "I know I mentioned that before, but it seems like San Francisco or Seattle or someplace like that would be a lot less dangerous for you."

I sighed and took out my wallet. Flipping through, I took out the creased photo I had inside. "Take a look," I said, handing over the photograph. "You may not recognize one of the people there, but that's me when I was twenty, about six months before I enlisted. The other people are my parents, my brother, Cain, and my sister, Denise. Once I was arrested, I've heard from them one time. My father wrote me a half-page letter that I got to read when I was in the holding brig at Fort Campbell awaiting my court martial. My defense JAG had asked my family to appear, to make a statement or something that could help my case. Instead, my father wrote back that neither he, my mother, or my siblings knew who Dane Bell was, and wanted no contact with said person forever. He disowned me, and disavowed that I'd ever been his son. It . . . it was difficult to read."

"Then why do you keep this photo?" Shawnie asked. "Isn't it painful?"

I nodded and took the photo back from Abby, tucking it back into my wallet. "Sometimes, our pain is what shapes us. I keep it because somewhere inside me is hope. Hope that some day, maybe I can redeem myself in my father's eyes, and I can be accepted back into my family. So far, though, no such luck."

"Have you tried to contact them?" Abby asked. "You were pretty determined to contact me."

"I write my parents every month," I said. "So far, all these years, every single one has been sent back marked 'Return to Sender.' I'll keep writing, though. Stamps are pretty cheap, and I don't have their email or Facebook accounts."

"And are you still living with Chris Lake?" Abby asked. "In that apartment?"

I nodded. "I am, but I have a job now, working at Lake Ford.

It's not much, just sweeping the repair bay and hauling stuff here and there, but it's a start. As soon as I can, I'm going to find my own place. The amenities may not be as nice, but I'll be standing on my own two feet again."

"Why'd you stay with Chris, anyway?" Shawnie asked. "I guess that also has something to do with Atlanta."

"Chris, Lloyd and I were in the same team in the 101st. Chris was our team leader. He'd enlisted nearly a year before I did. Afterward, he was the only guy who stayed in contact with me, and when he got out, he continued to send me the occasional letter. So after his father died and he inherited half-ownership of the Lake Automotive Group, he said that when I got out, to look him up in Atlanta. He's let me stay at that apartment, lent me some cash while I tried to find my own job, and when that didn't pan out, he hooked me up with the job at Lake Ford. Of all the people in the world, he was the only one who didn't toss me aside like a piece of trash after what happened to Lloyd. That's why."

Abby looked like she was about to say something about Chris, then closed her mouth. She looked down at the table, then at Shawnie, asking her a question without speaking swords.

"I think you've made up your mind already," Shawnie said with a smile. "On the good side, I've listened to every word he's said, and either he's been totally honest, or he's the world's best liar, in which case you spent the night with a sociopath."

I was still staring at the table when I felt the soft, sorely missed touch of her fingers on my hand, tenderly touching the back of it. I looked up to see Abby's eyes gazing into mine.

"Before you two get doe-eyed, I've got one more question, just for curiosity's sake," Shawnie said. "What'd you do all those years in prison?"

I looked over and smiled. "You have a lot of spare time, that's for sure. You can either spend it staring at the walls, staring at a television, or trying to better yourself. I tried to use my time to make myself better. Some studying and a lot of reading."

"Okay, I lied. One last thing, then I'll shut up. What sort of toppings do you think I should get for the tater tots that you're buying for me?"

I laughed and looked at the menu. "If it were up to me, I'd go with the chili and cheese."

"That seals it. You're a keeper," Shawnie said with a chuckle, patting Abby on the shoulder. "He has my seal of approval. You can kiss your boyf . . . whatever it is you want to call him."

"Actually, I had one more question," Abby said. "About Chris . . . how close are you two?"

The same look that was on her face when I mentioned Chris earlier came over her, and I tilted my head. I figured it was a bit of uncomfortableness over the fact that he and I were friends while he was an ex-boyfriend. Even if it had been years, there were rules that some people followed about that issue. "I owe him a lot. He gave me a home, a job, and loyalty when the rest of the world turned their backs on me. But, if you're worried about how he'd react, I think it wouldn't be a problem. He's moved on. Is it a problem?"

Abby shook her head, then lowered her head. "Dane, I feel like I have to say first that... "

She paused and was about to say something when a thunderous voice boomed across the tavern. "Abigail Melissa Rawlings!"

My head jerked up as Abby whipped her head around to see an older man, maybe in his late forties or early fifties, his eyes glaring at the two of us. He was in good shape for a man his age, and he had a vein pulsing in his forehead as he stood rooted to his spot, his hands clenched at his side. At the sight of him, Abby jerked her hands back from mine, her eyes wide and fearful. I surged out of my chair, getting in between the two while the tavern went dead quiet. "Who the hell . . .?"

"Dane, stop," Abby said quietly, laying her hand on my arm. "He's . . . he's my father. Daddy, this is—"

"I know who this son of a bitch is," Abby's father said. "I'll never forget the face of a goddamn terrorist sympathizing, murdering traitor. Dane-fucking-Bell."

"Daddy, please," Abby said, her voice quaking. "If you only knew him . . ."

"Enough!" he nearly screamed, his face turning purplish. "We're leaving. Now!"

I looked around the tavern. While there were a few people looking at Abby's father in shock and even some upset, there were just as many faces looking at me. Two of the guys looked like soldiers, perhaps on leave, or at least the type that wanted to be soldiers. High and tight haircuts, lean faces, and a look in their eyes that said they knew how to handle themselves. I reached back and put my hand on Abby's forearm, but not taking my eyes off her father. He looked mad enough to kill, and that was no exaggeration. "It's okay. It'd be better if

I go. Abby, thank you."

I left, trying to keep my head high, even as Abby's father stared daggers at me, along with a few of the other patrons. Shawnie saw what was going on and stood up, but I glanced back quickly and shook my head. Abby needed her friend more than I did.

Outside the tavern, I watched as Abby's father said something in her ear, and Shawnie tried to defend her friend before a glare from him silenced her as well. I saw the door to the tavern open, and the soldier boys started to come out.

I'm no coward, but this was one situation where discretion was the better part of valor. I couldn't help Abby, but messing with those two guys would get me nothing but time in jail. Hating every step, I left, walking just below a run back toward the apartment.

## Chapter 11

### Abby

When I heard Daddy's voice cut through the bar, I froze, my heart trembling in my chest as my head whipped around to see him standing there, rage on his face. I'd seen him that mad only once before, when Mike Burriss had been caught red-handed drunk on a job site, and his drinking had caused two other men to get hurt. Daddy had needed to be restrained by four other men that day, and I knew that I had to try and do something. If he'd attacked Dane, Dane would either catch a beating if he didn't fight back, or else Daddy would go to the hospital. I'd seen Dane fight, and for all my Dad's strength and rage, he wasn't a match.

Still, I also knew that Dane was a man who was conscious of his criminal record, and that he tried to do everything he could to blend in, not catch the attention of the police. If something did happen, he'd probably just let Daddy beat on him mercilessly. I had to do something, but I didn't know what. When Dane got up, trying to protect me, I laid a hand on his forearm, hoping that maybe I could use words to diffuse the situation. "Dane, stop. "He's . . . he's my father. Daddy, this is—"

Daddy cut me off, his face turning purplish and scaring me. After the cardiac incident back in high school, he wasn't supposed to get upset like this. And he almost never cut me off unless he was upset, and never by screaming at me. If anything, he would interrupt with quiet tones, never showing a lack of control of his emotions. He claimed it was what some of the upper-crust folks who tried to hold him back would use against him. This time, though, his voice was bellowing, loud, and dripping with the blue-collar accent that he'd tried his hardest in daily life to not let seep out. "Enough! We're leaving. Now!"

I wanted to say something more, but Dane's calm voice stopped me. I looked at him and was moved. He was obviously angry, but he was under control. A warm flush ran through me, knowing how much passion he had inside him, yet he kept it under such strong control— all to protect me. "It's okay. It'd be better if I go. Abby, thank you."

I watched Dane make his way out of The Nook, and turned my attention back to Daddy. "Daddy—"

"Abigail, not a damned word," he said, shocking me into silence. He had never, in my entire life, cursed at me. Sure, he might have occasionally described something in one of our conversations using a curse word, but never had he cursed *at* me. It brought tears to my eyes, and I gaped like a fish out of water, staring at him as he made his way to our table and grabbed the check. He wouldn't let a tab go unpaid, no matter how angry he was. "Get your things; we are leaving."

"Mr. Rawlings, please don't make a scene. Abby was trying to introduce you to him," Shawnie said, trying to be helpful. "If you'd only sit down and let her explain . . ."

He fixed Shawnie with a glare that could have melted through steel. I'd seen my friend stand up to harassing professors, ignorant frat boys, and even groups of people before, but under his eyes, she withered. She sat back down, her eyes barely still able to make contact with Daddy. "I have approved my daughter's friendship with you previously because she always described you as having a good head on your shoulders. Apparently, she was as mistaken in that as she was in talking to that bastard. Do not speak to me, and do not speak to my daughter ever again. Is that understood?"

Shawnie's a smart girl, and knew that trying to argue the point with him at that time would be futile. Instead, she was concerned with me, so she pulled her eyes away to look at me. "Are you going to be okay?"

"She'll be fine," Daddy said, his iron-hard grip on my arm pulling me toward the exit. There were a few of the customers who looked at me with concern, but no one wanted to get in our business. Not with the look in Daddy's eyes.

Outside, he let me go and pointed at his car, silent and resolute. He said nothing to me the whole time, the frame shaking as he slammed the door when he got in the car. He jammed the keys in the ignition, twisting them savagely until the starter whined and ground with the still-running engine, then stomping down on the accelerator so that his Escalade squealed rubber going out of the parking lot.

The whole time driving home, he was dead silent, the only sound in the car being the sound of his breath puffing in and out of his nose. I sat in the passenger seat, trying to figure out what to say, and couldn't. I was miserable, and there was nothing I could do about it. Ironically, the one thought going through my mind was what I'd have to do to get my car back, as it was parked in The Nook's lot. I wondered how long it would take for them to call a tow truck for it. I sighed and leaned my forehead against my window, wanting to cry but not allowing myself the bitter comfort of tears. I was stronger than that.

When we arrived home, Daddy parked the car and sat there,

trying to calm himself. "Abigail, I know that going to college, you get exposed to ideas that I may not agree with. And I accepted that. I'm not so backward and set in my ways that I'm afraid of your exposure to these ideas. I thought I'd raised you correctly, and that you would be able to discern the truth from the bullshit."

"But what I saw breaks my heart. It wasn't that you were talking to a traitor. Talking is one thing. But I saw the way you were holding his hand, and the way you were looking at him. You want to break my heart? You want to spit on everyone and everything I find important? Because that's what you did. A fucking traitor, Abby? What the hell's gotten into you?"

I couldn't help it. Long repressed tears spilled down my cheeks as I looked at the anguished face of my father. "Daddy, I'm sorry."

He shook his head and took out his keys. "Most days, that'd have been enough, Abby. But this . . . go to your room. Tomorrow, I'll take you to school for your tests. And I'll pick you up."

"Daddy, I'm grown. I can go to school on my own," I protested, and he looked back at me. "Besides, my car is parked at The Nook."

"Until I know I can trust you again, I don't think so. Now head to your room. You have tests tomorrow. I'll call the restaurant and make sure that your car is taken care of."

I followed his instructions, closing the door to my room behind me. Falling onto my bed, I let the rest of my tears out into my pillow. I wasn't sure if they were tears of rage, tears of sadness, tears of frustration, or what they were. I just knew they had to get out. I think it was mostly of anger, anger that I was being treated like a child. Either way, the tears were poisoning my body, my heart pounding in my chest and my eyes swelling to the point I could barely see, and I had to get them out.

I was just starting to gain control of myself when there was a knock on my bedroom door and Brittany came in. "Patrick has asked me to tell you that you're to have dinner in your room tonight, and that if you need anything, I'll be the person you should speak to," she said quietly, in a tone totally unlike her. It wasn't cold and it wasn't distant, like I'd expected. Instead, she sounded hollow. "He also asked me to collect your cellphone. He'd have me collect your laptop as well, except he thinks that you might need it for your studying."

"Brittany . . ." I said, then sighed and dropped my head. Reaching over, I grabbed my backpack and pulled out my smartphone, holding it out to her. "It isn't right."

For the first time I could think of, I saw frustration in Brittany's face while she took the phone from me and held it while she crossed her arms. I'd seen her piqued plenty of times, usually due to something I did, but I'd never seen this level of pure frustration before. She looked up to the ceiling and took a deep breath, then spoke. "You know, both of you are wrong in this instance. Maybe it's not my place to say it—but it's true."

"What do you mean?" I asked, shocked. I'd rarely heard Brittany talk in this way before, and I had certainly never heard her say something negative about Daddy. If she had ever criticized him, she must have done it just between the two of them.

"I mean, Abby, that Patrick is wrong in the way that he's handling this, while you were wrong to have met with that man in the first place. What do you even know about him?"

"A lot," I said, the fire building in my temper. I may not have inherited Daddy's size or physical strength, but I did inherit his stubbornness, even as much as I tried to control it. Sometimes that comes out as anger, whether I want it to or not. "He's not as bad as Daddy thinks he is. He's actually a good man, Brittany."

"That doesn't really matter now, does it?" Brittany asked. "You lied, Abby. Maybe not explicitly, but you lied by omission. Patrick and I both thought that your stress over the past month has been because of your upcoming finals and graduation. Now we find out that it was over some . . . some boy!"

"He's not a boy," I said simply. "If you saw him, you'd never say that again."

"You think that makes it sound any better?" Brittany asked. She held up her hand, silencing me. "Whatever the case may be, I suspect this has roots going all the way back to that morning you came home after staying out all night. I'm not going to give voice to my suspicions as to what happened that night, although I'm sure Patrick is thinking about the same thing."

I couldn't say anything but just dropped my head, unable to answer. Brittany sighed, then bonked her head against my door, a sound so natural and unlike her that I couldn't help it, smiling for an instant before disappearing into my other feelings. "That doesn't mean that Patrick has been blameless in his actions either, Abby. There was no reason for him to blow up at you like that, especially not in a public place. God knows what is going to happen to his account that he stormed out of."

I raised my head, surprised. "What are you talking about?"

133

Brittany huffed through her lips, pondering me for a second before answering. "Lake Automotive is looking at expanding, adding a heavy equipment dealership to their lineup. Patrick was meeting with Hank Lake to discuss the possibility of Rawlings Construction building it for them. As Hank is also a rather working-class man, they decided that a casual meeting over beers and some burgers was better than business suits and lawyers, at least at first."

It answered a question I'd had, and I let my breath escape in a whoosh. "So Daddy wasn't spying on me or following me."

Brittany chuckled darkly and shook her head. "No, he wasn't. You got caught by pure bad luck, Abby. Basically, at least according to what Patrick said to me, he looked around stretching, only to see you, your friend, and that man talking. He said something, and Hank looked up and remarked that it was . . . what's his name again?"

"Dane Bell," I answered hollowly.

Brittany clicked her fingers, nodding. "That's right. Dane Bell. In any case, you know your father. He never forgets something like that, and when he made the connection, he lost his temper."

"So what now?" I asked. "Brittany, I know you don't want to hear this, but I like Dane. A lot—"

"Just stop there," Brittany snapped, cutting me off. I closed my mouth, and she shook her head. "Just stop, please. I know what you want to say, and I'm not going to argue with you. If you're trying to get me to lessen your father's punishment on you, it won't work. But I do want peace in this house, and I do want us all to be a family. This past month, at least until tonight, has been some of the best for me and you, and I'd hope we could continue that. So don't throw a monkey wrench into that just yet. I'll talk with Patrick, see if he's willing to calm down. I do guarantee you that you will be taking that European History final tomorrow with him sitting in the parking lot—if not in the hallway outside the lecture hall. I guess the housing development in Douglas County will have to get along with just the foreman tomorrow."

Lessen my punishment? What am I, thirteen? Daddy's overprotectiveness was never really a problem until now. Things are starting to go a little too far. I'm a grown woman, and at some point, it has to stop.

"Then I guess I should get to studying," I said, sitting up. There was nothing more to say, and I just wanted to be left alone. "Thank you, Brittany."

She smiled, and I was struck at how pretty her smile was. I saw it so rarely, and it actually suited her. I wondered if she shared that smile with Daddy, and I hoped she did. "Don't stay up too late. Make sure you're well-rested for your test."

Brittany left, and I got out of my bed, going over to my little study desk and opening my laptop. She was right. I did have a test, and while I was still emotionally shattered, maybe I could get something else into my mind before trying to go to sleep. I fired up my Mac and went to my professor's course homepage, where the study notes were sitting organized and waiting for us.

I was just reviewing the ways the battle of Agincourt had changed warfare, and to a lesser degree, British culture, when I got a beep on my messenger program. I'd forgotten that I had it set to auto start whenever I booted up, and I wondered who it was. I was encouraged when I saw it was Shawnie.

*Hey, Shawnie.*

*Hey, Abby. I tried calling your phone, but you never picked up. I was worried.*

My friend's concern touched me, and I couldn't help but smile. *Daddy confiscated my phone as if I'm still a teenager. I'm still not okay, but I'm doing better than when I left The Nook. U?*

I had to wait a minute while Shawnie typed out her reply, during which I pulled up the Wikipedia on the Battle of Agincourt. If I was going to cram as much as I could last minute, going through the textbook just wasn't going to work. Besides, I only needed a B on the test.

Finally, Shawnie's reply popped up. *I got home okay. Wish I'd have been able to bum a ride like I'd planned, but the bus was cheap. I was thinking about calling the cops though. He was so mad . . .*

*It wasn't that bad, Shawnie. And before you start, I know I'm 22, I'm an adult, yada yada yada.* I threw in a couple of emojis, a shrugging one and a sheepish grin, then hit enter.

*Okay, but it's true. Actually, I had another question for you.*

*Go ahead,* I wrote. *I'm just perusing Agincourt.*

*Good, I hear it's always on the test. Anyway, I'll be blunt. What were you about to say before your dad yelled out? I hope you weren't going to say that you love him.*

It was my turn to sit back, thinking. Finally, I decided it was too late in Shawnie's and my relationship to lie. *I don't know.*

*Ok. Well, if you need my help, you got it.*

Good ol' Shawnie. I couldn't have asked for a better friend.

*Thanks. But for now, the main thing I need is to study. See you tomorrow morning.*

*Good night, Abby.*

\* \* \*

It took nearly a week, but eventually Daddy started to calm down and relax. I think part of it was when I showed him the results of my History final, an A minus that ensured that I would get on the Dean's List for my last semester as an undergrad. I got my phone back and was even *allowed* to attend my last few days by myself, without Daddy or Brittany taking me to campus like some sort of junior high school kid.

During that time, I texted Dane three times, the first to say that I was sorry about what happened, the second as a reply to his asking how I was doing, and the third just to see how he was doing. I didn't want my bad luck to rub off on him. I wanted to text more, but more than that, I wanted to hear his voice again. I just couldn't take the risk though, as desperate as I was. I wasn't sure I could control myself if I did.

The fact was, other than when I was studying or in the tests themselves, I was constantly thinking about Dane. I'd just finished my last final, the defense of my capstone project with the head of the biology department when my phone rang and I saw that it was an unknown number. A wild idea flashed through my mind, and I answered the phone, hoping that it was Dane calling from a new phone or something. "Hello?"

"Hi, Abby, it's Chris Lake," Chris said, disappointing me, but at the same time setting loose a wild idea in my mind. "How're you doing?"

Chris sounded like he hadn't heard about my little incident at

137

The Nook, so I assumed that Dane hadn't told him, nor had his uncle. If they hadn't, I figured there was no reason for me to either. "I'm doing okay, Chris. Just finished my last final. How about you?"

I could hear him chuckle, but again, there was that sense of something different that I'd felt when I saw him smile the time I'd given him my phone number. It was like I was listening to a stranger, and not the guy I'd dated five years earlier. Most disturbing, though, was that whoever Chris had become, he wasn't exactly someone I was interested in. "I'm doing well. I just closed a pretty big investment property deal and was looking to celebrate. I was thinking of getting together with some people, and wondered if you'd like to come with me. Nothing major, it's not a date or anything, but just a bit of a party out at the site of the deal."

"Oh? What sort of site?" I asked, curious if nothing else. It wasn't that I didn't like Chris. I just wasn't interested in him. Besides, while it'd require my lying to Daddy, seeing Dane would be worth it.

"I just closed the deal on a housing development on Blalock Reservoir," Chris said. "It's a little south of Atlanta, near Jonesboro. Do you know it?"

"I've been down there a few times," I said honestly. It had been years, but Daddy had taken me down there to do some fishing, just for fun. "It's a nice little area. I think the last time I was down there, we went to Lake Spivey. That's nearby, right?"

"Right. Well, we just signed a deal with the Clayton County Water Authority that's going to allow us to put in a whole development down there. The land actually already has a lake house. That's where the party's going to be."

My idea started to sound more and more plausible, and I couldn't help it. I smiled. "Sounds like fun. When's the party going to be?"

My smile must have come through in my voice, because Chris sounded a lot more excited than he had at the beginning of the call. "Saturday at noon. What do you say?"

Wild hope flared in my chest, and I answered quickly. "I'll see what I can do. Can you text me directions? Daddy's been a bit protective, and he's not going to like a man coming around the house and calling on me right now."

"That sounds like the Patrick I remember. Okay, I'll send them to you. And bring your swimsuit if you'd like. I think someone's going to bring their boat, and there might be some tubing at least."

"I might do that. See you later, Chris."

"See you later, Abby. Bye."

I headed toward my car when I heard Shawnie call my name. I turned around, waving. "Hey, Shawnie! What're you doing here? I thought your last class was yesterday."

My friend came closer, shaking her head, the long ringlet curls of her hair bouncing with every motion. "You're right, but did you really think I was going to let you defend your capstone without me at least checking on you? Besides, in the last week I've barely seen you. At least, not without a parental shadow. How're you doing?"

I took out my car keys and unlocked the door. "Tell you what: we can talk while I give you a ride back to your place or something. I owe you that much after The Nook."

"I'll always take a free ride," Shawnie said, going around and

139

climbing into the passenger seat. She hissed when her mostly-bare legs hit the dark leather seats of the Camaro that I'd gotten as a high school graduation present, and I noticed she was wearing kinda short shorts. She pulled her knees up and rubbed the backs of her legs. "I keep forgetting about these damn seats."

"Don't worry, my A/C is super blasting," I replied, turning on the engine and cranking the cold air. Within seconds, we could already feel a difference, and I put my car into reverse and backed out of my parking spot. "Hey, I just had a call and a crazy idea, and I was wondering if I could run it past you."

"Go ahead, I love crazy ideas. The Wright Brothers were batshit insane for their day," Shawnie said, slowly lowering her legs to the leather with a contented sigh. "After all, so were a lot of the most famous aeronautical engineers."

I was stunned for a second, not sure what the hell to say to that, when I just waved it off. "Well, I just got a call from Chris Lake. You remember the name, right?"

Shawnie nodded as I turned right and headed north toward her apartment. "Yeah, your ex-boyfriend who also knows Dane, and you ran into a little while back. By the way, you're beginning to sound like a soap opera with this love life of yours. What's up with him?"

"Well, he invited me to a lake party this Saturday, and I was kind of thinking of doing a little rope-a-dope. Shawnie, I've really got to see Dane, but with Daddy all up in my business, I need some help."

Shawnie grinned and tapped a quick beat on the dashboard of my car in front of her. "I like it. What's your idea?"

\* \* \*

When Daddy got home from the office that night, he found me relaxing in the TV room, stretched out on the couch. He gave me a smile, something that I hadn't realized I missed until we went days without his being anything but angry at me. "Well now, Abby girl, how did it go?"

"I'll find out in two days. But I think it went really well. If it did as well as I think, I'll be sure to get into the GT Master's program. Also, I had an interesting phone call."

"Oh?" Daddy said, unable to contain his excitement. He had always been supportive of my academic pursuits, as he felt that education was the key to a better life than what he'd built. "And what was that?"

I sat up, trying my best to put on a cute expression for him. I don't normally turn on the charm on him, but I just had to this time. "Well, Daddy, do you remember Chris Lake? You know, of Lake Automotive?"

"Of course, baby. You and he dated back when you were a senior in high school. If I remember right, you were pretty down when you guys broke up. I never understood why either."

I shrugged, playing it off. I didn't have time to explain it, and besides, it didn't matter. Chris was my past. I was more interested in my future. "I dunno. But, I ran into him the other day, and he's doing really well for himself. He's taken over half of Lake Automotive, and he's got his own real estate company now too."

He looked impressed, though he probably already knew that, and if I wasn't so focused on my plan to try and meet Dane, I would have been upset. "Good for him. I always thought he was a good boy.

Although he'd be what, twenty-eight, twenty-nine now?"

"I think twenty-nine," I said quickly, trying to advance the conversation. "Anyway, I got a call from Chris today. His real estate company just closed a big deal out on Blalock Reservoir, and he invited me to a company barbecue party to celebrate the deal this Saturday. I thought if I went, maybe he would keep you in mind when it came time for the actual construction of his project."

"Wheelin' and dealin' for me, baby? I don't need that," Daddy said, but I could see him smile despite himself. He tried, but he worried too much about me, including the size of my bank account once he passed on. A good marriage, in his opinion, was essential to that. "What about Chris himself? Like I said, I remember you two were pretty sweet on each other."

"That was a while back, but yes, I liked Chris a lot. Besides, I thought a bit of a lake party would be fun, and let me de-stress after all of this. And it's not like its going to be some sort of wild college party or anything. Probably a lot of polo shirts and khakis, I bet."

He sat down in his easy chair and started to sit back, then stopped. "Wait. I remember when I was talking to Hank Lake—Dane Bell is living with Chris."

"Really? I didn't know," I lied through my teeth, pretty convincingly. Inside of me, I felt a little twinge, but that twinge quickly went away. "I just wanted to go to the party, that's all."

He studied me for a moment, then nodded. "Okay. You're a big girl now. I'll give my permission. But, there's one condition."

I rolled my eyes but tried my best to hide it. He'd just said I was a big girl, then followed it up with *he'll give his permission with a condition.*

"What's that, Daddy?" I asked, trying not to get up and cheer.

"Chris is a good man, but he's loyal to a fault. If he goes all noble or anything and invites that traitor, Dane Bell, you are not to hang out or even talk to him. If he approaches you, you politely inform him that you are not to speak with him, and you go on your way. I will not tolerate you and him spending time together, Abby. Understand me?"

I nodded and prepared to give him a big lie for the first time in my life. "I promise. If Dane Bell is at the party, I will not speak to or hang out with him."

## Chapter 12

## Dane

I was sitting in the park on the grass overlooking the pond, relaxing after a long day at work, content if not wildly happy. After the incident at The Nook, I'd worried about three things. First, that Abby was okay. Second, that she still wanted to see me. We'd had such a great conversation and connected at the end. I needed just a few more minutes, and to be honest, I was actually angry about it. Thankfully, before I went to sleep, I saw that Abby had sent me a text message that she was okay and that she would talk to me when she had the chance.

However, there was a third concern that left me sleepless for the rest of the night. I just couldn't help but think I was going to walk into work at Lake Ford and find myself terminated. When Hank Lake called me into his office the next morning, I was sure of it. I hadn't even started my shift yet.

"You wanted to see me, Mr. Lake?" I asked, mentally debating if I was willing to debase myself enough to beg for my job, or at least ask to finish out the day. I could have used the money.

Hank looked up from his chair, noticing that I was at least in clean clothes, my coveralls freshly washed and still actually smelling slightly of fabric softener. "Yeah, Bell. I just wanted to tell you that what I saw last night, stays last night. To be honest, I was impressed at how calm you stayed."

I was stunned. Recovering quickly, I found my voice. "Thank you, sir. I apologize if I caused any trouble."

Hank shook his head. "Not at all. I've met Abby Rawlings before. She's a beautiful young woman. Of course, I assume you know that she and Chris were involved before."

I nodded. "Yes sir. But when I met Abby, I didn't know that. When we were in the service, Chris never told me her name. It wasn't until later that the connection was made."

Hank tapped his desk, pondering for a moment before shrugging and continuing. "I see. Well, that's not here nor there, I'd prefer to stay out of that issue. In any case, I just wanted to let you know. By the way, I saw you weren't scheduled for the weekend this week. Planning on enjoying the time off?"

It was my turn to shrug, as I was still flummoxed from the past thirty seconds of conversation. "I was thinking I might look at some apartments if I get the chance. I'm not quite ready yet, but I'm itching to stand on my own. I looked in the paper and saw a few cheap places that don't need a big deposit."

"Most likely in neighborhoods where you're going to be putting that military training of yours to daily use," Hank said with a laugh, tossing his pen onto his desk, where it clattered before coming to rest on his blotter. "All right, I'm not going to tell a man not to be a man. If you need a reference or anything, give them my number."

That conversation had calmed my last fear, and the rest of the week went well. Now, on Friday night, I was in the park relaxing after work not because of lack of funds, but because when I came back to the Tower, I found a tie hanging on the doorknob of the apartment. Holding my ear to the door confirmed that Chris did have some female companion over, a quite vocal one at that. I figured tonight would be a good night to just chill out, and backed away from the door, trying to figure out what I wanted to do with the rest of my evening. From the sounds of it, Chris and the lady were enjoying each other's company, and I'd need plans until at least midnight, if not morning.

Thankfully, unlike some of the guys in the shop who wore their work clothes to and from work, I used the locker room. So while my clothes weren't exactly dressy, they wouldn't get me kicked out of an Applebee's either.

The sun was still low on the horizon and the sky was golden when my phone rang, and I opened it up to see Abby's name on the caller ID. "Abby?"

"Hi, Dane," she said, her voice sounding a bit nervous. "How are you doing?"

"Pretty good, but the past five seconds have been the best part of my day," I replied honestly. "It's good to hear your voice again."

"You too," she said. "I know this sounds weird and all, but I was really hoping I could see you again tomorrow. Daddy won't know."

I should have said no. I knew it. I should have said that if we were going to see each other, then we had to be honest with her father, even if it meant that he would be pissed off. I should have, but I didn't. Instead, I let my lust do the talking, which said that if I had to make my way through a mile of rabid pit bulls to see this woman, I would. "Of course. I have the day off, lucky for me. What do you want to do?"

"How about you meet me at the Midtown MARTA station?" Abby asked. "And dress casual. It'll be a surprise. I'll be honest, I'm kind of making this up as I talk."

"Deal," I said, leaning back and just relishing the sound of her voice in my ear. "Abby, are you going to get in trouble for this?"

"Sometimes things are worth getting in trouble for," she said softly. "I didn't understand that before . . . but I think I do now."

"I know what you mean," I said, sitting up on the grass and watching a couple of kids throwing a Frisbee back and forth. "Abby, you're causing a lot of emotional changes in me. Some of them are pretty scary, actually."

I could hear the smile in her voice as she replied, but still, a trace of nervousness clung to her honeyed tones. "Really? Like what?"

"Like for the first time since I can remember, I think there might be a chance that I could find real happiness in life," I said. "Like maybe I'm not just a barely tolerated dog in the world, to be kicked and smacked around until I lose it and bite back. Like maybe there is someone for me, and that there might be a chance at . . . well . . ."

"At what?" she asked, her breath caught in her throat. I could tell she wanted me to say it, but I didn't want to say it prematurely. We still had a while to go.

"At love," I finally said in a whisper. I ran my hand through my hair and laughed. "Is that too much to hope for?"

"No." Abby's answer came back at nearly the same level of whisper that I had used. "I feel the same way. I don't know if that's what this is, but I have hope."

* * *

The next day, I waited outside the Midtown MARTA station when a white Chevy Camaro pulled up and Abby waved. I hurried over, jumping in on the passenger side. Looking around the interior, I ran my hand over the real leather, impressed. Maybe it was living in the Mayfair Tower, maybe it was that I had a job of my own now, but I had come to be able to appreciate the trappings of Abby's economic status without being too worried about my position relative to them. "Wow, this is a great car."

"Thanks," Abby said. I couldn't help it—I stared at her as she pulled out. She was wearing jean shorts, not quite short shorts but damn close, with what I was sure was about a mile and a half of toned, beautifully tanned leg sticking out, along with a blue tank top and her hair pulled back into a thick, braided ponytail that completed the package. I could feel blood begin to rush to my cock, and I could only sit there like an idiot. When we got to the stop light, she looked over at me and smiled shyly. "You're staring. And not wearing your seat belt."

"Sorry," I replied, jerking my eyes away and putting on my belt. "Just . . . you look beautiful today. So what is on your agenda?"

Abby's smile was contagious, and she jerked a thumb behind her. I looked and saw the folded bulge of a blanket and a picnic basket. "I guess you can tell, but I'm an outdoors-type girl, and I couldn't think of anything better than having a picnic with my boyfriend."

"Is that what we are now?" I asked. I tried to think back to the last time a girl had called me her boyfriend, and I realized it was nearly a decade prior, back when I'd just gotten out of high school. Of course, I'd had plenty of hookups since then, at least before Iraq, but never had I been someone's boyfriend. "Are you sure about that? I'm not the most popular guy around here."

Abby got on I-85 and headed north, letting the horses under the hood of her car walk it out some. I wasn't sure exactly what she had, except that it was one of the newer Camaros, but I doubted she was running a factory standard motor under the hood. I'd heard enough engines in the near month that I was working at Lake Ford to know a tuned up car when I heard it. "I'm positive," she said as she smoothly merged. "After today, I was thinking that no matter what, I'm going to tell Daddy we're going to see each other. He'll be so pissed off at me that I lied to him, but I don't care. After last week, I have to follow my heart, and it's time for me to put a stop to him controlling my life. I've let it go on for so long that it has become second-nature to him."

"So what did you tell him, anyway?" I asked, curious. I wanted to say something else, but didn't have the words just yet. "Just so that when he kicks in my door with his twelve-gauge ready, I'll know what to say."

"Oh, he doesn't have a twelve-gauge," Abby said, then looked over at me. "He's got a ten-gauge."

I rolled my eyes, laughing. "Even worse. Although I guess it means more mess for the coroner to pick up. It's worth it, though. So what did you tell him?"

"Well, I was invited to a party by Chris Lake," she said, "down near the reservoir. Anyway, I didn't tell him flat out yes, but I did arrange for Shawnie to go in my place. She's going to say that I invited her too, and that I would meet her there. If Chris asks, I'll tell him that I had car trouble or something. Daddy doesn't need to know more about it, except that you and I were together instead of at the party like I'd originally told him."

The way she said *together* sent shivers down my spine, and I hummed, half nervously. "So, we're lying to both your father and to the man who is giving me a place to stay. This sounds like a dangerous game."

"I'm willing to take the plunge if you are," Abby said. It was easy for her to say. She had never really experienced any consequences in her life. Not that I wasn't in—I was all in—but I wasn't sure if she would stick to it once the going got tough.

"Dane . . . my feelings for you are hard to put words to."

"Then let's wait until we get to wherever it is you're taking us," I said. "It's probably safer to drive when you're not searching for words."

We left Atlanta, heading out into the suburbs, until Abby took an off-ramp and drove me down a few winding roads to the side of a river. "I thought about a park. I even thought about us going to Six Flags, but I decided that I wanted something more private."

"Even better," I said amiably as I got the picnic basket and blanket out of the back. "Ooof, this thing weighs a ton. What all do you have in here?"

"You're a big man, with big appetites," Abby teased, her meaning very clear. "I wanted to make sure we were both satiated today."

Abby led me down a narrow path to a clearing, where I spread out the blanket. "What is this place?"

"Just a fishing spot that Daddy and I would sometimes go to when the creek at the house was boring," Abby said. "It's special to him because it's the spot where he and Mom got engaged."

Abby spread out the blanket underneath a huge magnolia tree, the shadows from the wide leaves giving us plenty of shade. "It's beautiful today," she said as I took a seat.

"Abby, can I ask you a question?"

"Of course. Shoot." Abby opened the basket and took out a sub sandwich wrapped in butcher paper. It was easily a foot long, and about as big around as my forearm. It looked like it could have fed a horse. "Sorry. I would have come up with something more homemade, but it would have looked funny. Thankfully, the picnic basket was in the garage, or else we'd be eating our picnic out of a plastic shopping bag."

"This is just fine," I said, unwrapping it to find a turkey sub with bacon and cranberry mustard dressing. Easily a half pound of turkey slices, probably an entire pack of bacon, and just a bit of cheese complimented the whole package. "It's a little Thanksgiving, isn't it?"

"You can always enjoy a good Thanksgiving," Abby said, taking out a can of Pringles and a bottle of Cheerwine. She handed them to me, then got her own, much smaller sandwich and sides out, along with the same Cheerwine. When I looked at her bottle, she raised it in a salute. "A Southern tradition, you know."

"I love it," I answered, toasting her and opening both bottles. "I guess my question is, what happens next?"

"What do you mean, next?" Abby asked carefully, setting her bottle down. "Do you mean with me going to grad school? Well, I'm planning on going to GT for my Masters too, and after that, well, we'll just have to see. What do you think of North Carolina? Duke and UNC both have great Ph.D. programs."

"Last time I went to North Carolina, it was on leave," I said, thinking back into my memories. "I ran into some boys from the 82nd.

When they found out I was 101st, we had a *friendly* discussion that ended up with my getting a black eye."

Abby laughed and sighed. "That's what I like about you, Dane."

"What?" I asked, taking a huge bite out of my sandwich. It was juicy and delicious, and I reminded myself to get the address of the shop from Abby, no matter what. "That I got my ass kicked? I mean, I gave as good as I got against three other guys, but that's beside the point."

"No, that you're secure enough in who you are and in your maturity that you're willing to admit that. Any other man I've ever met, after the way we met, at least, would have told me a litany of lies that made him look like the world's biggest badass," she said, laying back on the blanket and letting her body stretch out. She looked so sexy, I couldn't have taken my eyes from her anyway. "You're the real deal, and you don't try to flaunt it. It's refreshing. And you know what else?"

"What?" I asked.

"I'm hoping that you're going to take advantage of our privacy and this blanket," she purred, cupping her breast. "I've not been able to get that night out of my mind for six weeks. If that's what you meant by what's next."

It wasn't, but I damn sure wouldn't turn something like that down. Setting the delicious food aside, I lifted the basket out of the way, making sure it was clear of anything before I lay down next to Abby, pulling her into my arms and softly kissing her lips.

I tasted the sweet wine on her mouth and tongue. Her breasts pushed up into my chest, and her legs were warm and strong under mine. Abby's kiss was tender and loving, her fingers running through my hair and pulling me in tighter.

With a giggle and a squeal, we rolled until she was on top, kissing me with her hair dangling over our face. Breaking our kiss, she traced my forehead and eyebrows, looking down on me. "Dane."

"Yes, Abby?" I asked as she wiggled her body, rubbing against my now raging hard on.

"Call me Abs. You're the first person to ever do that, and . . . well . . . I kinda like it."

My answering combined chuckle and moan was more than enough of an answer, and we kissed again, my hands going from caressing to demanding, hungry to feel the silky smoothness of Abby's skin and to see her nude in the shaded afternoon light. "Abs." It came so naturally.

She lifted her body enough for me to pull her tank top up and off, leaving her in just a lacy bra. I repeated the name over and over, kissing down her throat and finding her pulse on her collarbone. She mewled and gasped, struggling to form a question. "Please, can you take off your things too?"

"Please? I like that," I teased, letting her get off me while I sat up. I'd dressed casually, but still more than she had, with a light cotton, button-down shirt to go with my own cargo shorts, five years or more out of fashion, but what I was still comfortable with.

She reached for the button on her shorts at the same time, and I noticed that her bra had a front clasp this time. I wondered if she had planned on seducing me even as we had talked the evening before. I couldn't complain. I'd hoped for it either way. She saw where my eyes were fixed and raised an eyebrow, unclasping the bra and letting her perfect, heavy teardrops expose to the air and to my view. I reached up, cupping one of her breasts and letting it rest in my hand. "You certainly like these."

"How could I not?" I replied, taking my hand away and undoing my shorts. I pushed them down, glad I'd worn the Nikes instead of boots, as I could pull my shorts off easily. "Sorry, forgot the shoes."

"I don't care," Abby said, reaching for my cock. "This is what I've been desperate to have."

"I'm just a big cock life support unit then?" I teased, causing her to stop and smile.

"Oh you're a little more than that," she teased. "But yes, you sure know how to use it," she said with my dick in her hand. "And there's something I've wanted to do that I didn't last time."

"Oh?" I asked, thinking back to the night in the apartment. It was hard to concentrate when I had a beautiful woman stroking my cock with her small, perfect hand, and my thoughts were totally blown away when she quickly knelt and took the head of my cock in her mouth, sucking and licking the sensitive tip.

Abby's lips sealed around my shaft added to the sensation, and I knew if she kept that up, I was going to fill her mouth with my come before she even got all the way down. Reaching forward, my hand traveled over the smooth curve of her backside, noticing that she'd lost a few pounds since our first night. It must have been the stress of studying, I thought, but I didn't mind. She was perfect no matter what, and as my fingers reached between her butt cheeks to find the warm moistness of her cleft, I shuddered as she groaned around me.

I stayed there for as long as I could, Abby slowly bobbing her head on my cock while I rubbed my fingers over the edges of her lips. Finally, I couldn't resist it anymore and I pulled back, grabbing her ponytail and pulling her up into a searing kiss. Our lips were hot and liquid, flowing over each other and sucking hard while we growled. Our inner feral natures were coming out, and this beautiful woman was more than willing to match my inner nature with her own passion.

"Give it to me, Dane," Abby hissed at me as her fingers pulled at the muscles along my shoulders and neck. "Show me what you can do."

Her words stirred my passion to flaming heights, and I pushed her back onto the blanket, her legs wrapping around me as I claimed her mouth with mine again. Reaching down, I aligned myself with her wet entrance and pushed in, not too fast, but unrelenting. If she wanted to be my woman, she would be *my* woman.

Abby didn't make a single sound of complaint as I sank my entire length into her. A warm moan started deep in her chest as I pushed farther and farther in, until my balls rested on the curve of her ass below me. Pulling back, I looked into her sapphire eyes, which were wide with amazement and pleasure. Tracing my hand over her heart, I let loose the words of my heart. "You're going to be mine—forever."

She smiled, bringing her hand up to rest over my heart, her voice thick and syrupy with desire. I pulled back and drove into her again. Shudders rippled through her body with the feeling. We fell into a fast, hungry pace, demanding from each other everything the other had. My right hand was still wrapped with her ponytail as I drove into her over and over, our eyes locked on each other as our passion built. I'd never found a woman like Abby before, whose genuine desire matched my own in perfect harmony, rising to meet me and pulling me in for more and more.

My orgasm built quickly within me, and I didn't care. I could tell she was on the edge as well. I knew it—and knew there would be other times for gentleness and tenderness. This was about laying claim to each other. I was determined to make her mine.

Faster and faster, my hips rose and fell while I pinned Abby to the blanket, my hand tight in her hair and her fingers raking down my back. I felt the steely fire of my skin tearing as her fingernails cut furrows in my back, but the pain fueled my passion even more, and my hips pounded into her even harder. "Yes, yes, yes," she cried, biting her lower lip. "Fuck me!"

We raced each other toward our orgasm, my body trembling and covered in sweat from the exertion and the heat of the early summer day. With a trembling growl, I plunged my cock into her one more time, her legs tightening as Abby's orgasm swept through her, her fingers digging in harder than they ever had. The feeling of her pussy clenching and massaging my cock that last time was the trigger I needed, and I exploded, letting out a powerful, feral growl.

When I was finally done, and my body relaxed into the boneless happiness that is the wonder of a post-orgasm glow, I leaned down, kissing Abby tenderly and rolling both of us onto our sides. "I think I'm falling in love with you, Abs."

"Me too, *Dene*," she said. When I cocked an eyebrow, she smiled and traced my face with her fingertips. "In my studies, I ran across the word that the old English used for the Viking warriors. They called them *Dene*, or what eventually became Dane. I thought it appropriate for you."

I kissed her softly, my heart warming. "It's fitting, given what I've turned to religiously. I'll treasure it, Abs. Maybe I can get it tattooed on my body somewhere."

"I was thinking of maybe having it tattooed on mine," Abby replied with a smile. "And what do you mean? Are you into Norse mythology or something?"

I shrugged and shook my head. "I don't know—kind of. I started looking for something to believe in after my conviction. But it started a little before that."

"Tell me about it," Abby said softly, rolling back and pillowing her head on her arm. "I want to know everything about you, even the dark parts."

I nodded and rolled onto my stomach, tenting my chin on my hands and looking out at the river beyond. "I guess part of it was my upbringing. My family was one of those weekly churchgoing families— every Sunday, like clockwork. But there was nothing happening despite all that praying. It continued in the Army, as some of the biggest assholes I knew were also some of the most churchgoing. Still, I tried to keep at least a little bit of faith, but after what happened in Iraq, I practically gave up on it. So I thought about it, and I picked Norse mythology because it seemed to fit what I was going through. It's a religion where everything pretty much goes to hell, and the good guys get screwed in a major way. Kinda fit in with my outlook on life back then."

"And now?" Abby asked. "Do you still think that life sucks and then you die?"

I rolled to my side and kissed her nose, shaking my head. "I don't know for sure, but things do seem to have taken a turn for the better."

## Chapter 13

### Abby

Unfortunately for our desires, regardless of how long we wanted to stay there, I had to go home eventually. As it was, we stayed until the sun started to go down, then had a casual dinner at a little country barbecue place. "I never realized just how voracious an appetite you have," I said as he came back from the buffet with his third plate. "Have you been starving yourself or something?"

Dane grinned and shook his head. "No, but I did work up quite an appetite this afternoon. And it's a bit of an old habit that I've not quite worked past yet."

"What's that?" I asked, enjoying the rich pork myself.

"Until recently, I mostly just ate to live," Dane said simply as he used his plastic fork to split a biscuit in half. He took forkfuls of the spicy barbecue and put it on the halves, making an open-faced sandwich that he started consuming in efficient, neat bites. Despite it being his third plate, and the barbecue being soaked in nearly an obscene amount of sauce, his shirt was spotless, a far cry from my own.

"Luxury for my family was getting eighty-twenty ground beef to go into our mac & cheese casserole. The Army was the same way, and Leavenworth . . . well, you can guess what that was like. In any case, during all that time, I ate enough to not be hungry, but I hated a lot of what I had to put in my mouth. On the rare occasions that I was able to have delicious food, I ate as quickly and as much as I could. I never knew when I'd get another chance to indulge in it again."

"Well, now that you won't have that issue, it's a habit I suggest you look at breaking unless you want to end up the size of a small elephant," I teased.

Dane immediately set his fork down and pushed his plate away. "Well, I'm still going to have some Key Lime Pie."

I couldn't help it. I laughed. "Dane, I'm not saying don't enjoy tonight. It's actually kind of cute to watch. You act like a man, a real man. I've spent too many meals surrounded by frat boys who worry about their six-packs and their haircuts. So enjoy. I guess what I was trying to say, not too successfully, is that your life isn't that way anymore, and you don't have to worry about it."

Dane thought about it, teasing the pile of barbecue with his fork. "Abs, we seem to have something going here, but I don't want to be a kept man. I never have been and never will be."

I blushed and looked down, twisting my napkin until it started to tear. "I'm sorry, I didn't mean that either. I'm just trying to say, money isn't important to me. And I'm not going to live off of Daddy for the rest of my life—something I should have started already. I'll admit, I'm self-centered, I'm greedy, and I'm spoiled rotten. In other words, I'm your normal girl."

Dane laughed and pulled his plate closer. "You are far from normal. In fact, you're pretty exceptional."

* * *

When I got home, Daddy and Brittany were enjoying a movie together in the family room, looking comfortable together. I hadn't seen them like that often before, and I had to admit that it was nice to see. They looked like a normal couple. "I'm back."

"Did you have fun, sweetie?" Brittany asked, leaning against Daddy.

"I did. The water was nice," I lied. "How about you guys?"

"We had a good afternoon," Daddy said. "You want to join us? *Blazing Saddles* is coming on in a few minutes."

I shook my head, tired after the warmth and the day's exertions. "No thanks. I'm pretty worn out. I think I'll get a bath and go to sleep, if y'all don't mind."

I rarely let a y'all slip out. Brittany usually corrected me on it, but this time she was content, and I think our conversation a few days earlier helped. She waved from the couch, not even looking up from her position nestled next to Daddy to worry about it. "All right, Abby. See you in the morning."

Up in my room, I noticed that my phone was blinking, meaning I had some messages or missed calls. I'd ignored it all day, in fact leaving it in my bag in the car while Dane and I spent the afternoon together. I turned it on, surprised to see over a dozen missed calls.

Checking my call log, I was a little worried to see that ten of the missed calls were from Chris, with two from Shawnie. Also, there were three messages from Chris to my phone.

*Party's just getting started, I hope you get here soon!*

*Hey, where are you? Your friend got here, hope you can join us!*

*At least give me a call, or tell me what's going on.*

It was the tone of the last message that concerned me. I just got a sense that Chris seemed to expect something, and I thought about giving him a call to clear things up. I hope he didn't get the idea that I wanted to see him again. It was nearly nine, though, and I decided to give Shawnie a call instead. She picked up almost any time of the day or night.

Shawnie's phone rang over and over, and I grew concerned. She usually turned her phone off if she couldn't answer. This time, though, her phone just kept ringing, until finally it kicked over to her voice mail. "Hey, Shawnie, it's me. Just wanted to see how you were doing. I saw you tried to call. I'm a bit concerned—you normally have your phone set differently. Gimme a call if you can and tell me how the party went. Talk to you later, bye."

I repeated the message in a text and put my phone on its charger. Yawning, I realized I really was tired, and I changed out of my clothes into some sleep shorts and a pajama top and climbed into bed. Dreams of Dane and me making love on the side of the river warmed me throughout the night, and I woke up feeling better than I had in a long time. I knew that my dream had to have good meaning for the day ahead, and I planned again how I was going to approach Daddy about everything involving Dane.

Taking my phone from the charger, concern swept back over me when I saw that Shawnie hadn't messaged me back. It was already nearly ten in the morning, and she had always been a notoriously early riser—to the point of annoying me more than once with her seven in the morning perkiness. I enjoyed sleeping in when I didn't have to be up, and after the physical exertion of the night before, I was more than ready to crash for a whole day.

I quickly showered and changed clothes, pulling on some jeans and a t-shirt. Going into the kitchen, I saw Daddy drinking his morning green tea as he read a spy novel, a habit he had picked up at my urging. Considering the time, it was probably his second cup of the day before he enjoyed his Saturday morning. "How did you sleep, sweetheart?"

"I'm fine, Daddy, but I need to go run an errand," I said, grabbing my car keys. "I hope it won't take too long."

"What is it, honey?" he asked, setting his tea and book down to look at me. "

"My friend, Shawnie. She didn't answer her phone or the text message I sent her last night. I'm just a bit worried about her, and I want to make sure she's okay."

I had expected him to protest, but he waved it off. Instead, he picked up his paperback and took another sip of his tea. "I was a bit too harsh on her, I think. You two have been friends for a long time, and I shouldn't have taken out my concerns on her. Besides, from what you said the other night, you won't be seeing much of each other soon, and I don't want to stop you from having some good memories."

"Thanks, Daddy," I said, going over and giving him a kiss on the cheek. "I'll see you in a bit."

Jumping in my car, I thought about calling Dane, but I decided I was being silly. Instead, I sent him a text message. *I didn't have a chance to talk to Daddy yet. But I will.*

He replied quickly, and I snuck a look while waiting at a red light. *It's okay. I know it needs to be done, but I'm not looking forward to that one anyway. I'm going to go out apartment hunting. Talk to you in a while.*

His reply made me smile, and I turned left toward Shawnie's

neighborhood. Being on a scholarship and not exactly coming from means, Shawnie's apartment wasn't in the best part of Atlanta.

Pulling up in front of Shawnie's place, I didn't see her car at all. Not answering her phone was one thing if she were home, but Shawnie was as much a smartphone junkie as I was—she never left without it. Still, I parked my car in her space and went up to her apartment, knocking on the door. "Hello?"

A young woman, about Shawnie's age, opened the door. "May I help you?"

"Hi," I said, a bit confused. I hadn't met the girl before, and I felt a bit taken aback. Then again, Shawnie frequently changed roommates, letting anyone who wasn't doing drugs, and had the money, crash to share the rent. "My name's Abby. I'm a friend of Shawnie's. Is she home right now?"

The thick accent of the girl was something that I'd heard a lot of, and told me that while she was staying in Shawnie's apartment for now, she probably wouldn't be for long. "Naw, Shawnie ain't been back since yesterday. Said she had some lake party or somethin' she was goin' to."

"Oh, okay. I guess I'll try her phone again," I said. "It was just something to do with classes. Thanks."

The girl nodded and closed the door quietly, leaving me standing on the walkway in front, still confused. I pulled out my phone and tried Shawnie again, but hung up when she didn't pick up after the fifth ring. Going back to my car, I thought about what may have happened. "Maybe Shawnie followed my lead and found a cute guy," I said to myself while the air conditioning blasted. "I mean, she's single, cute, and likes men. No reason she can't have a little summer lovin' before heading out west."

Still, it didn't jive with me. Shawnie having a hook-up, I could understand. After all, I'd basically done the same thing. But Shawnie having a hook-up and not sending me a message or replying to what I sent her? That I didn't see happening.

"I should check in with Chris," I said to myself again. "He may be pissed that I ditched his party, but maybe I can find out who was there, and if Shawnie hooked up with someone."

Nodding at my logic, I stopped to send another little text to Dane asking about the apartment search. He replied almost immediately. *I've got one more to check out, then I'm going back to the apartment.*

His words let me calm my nerves enough to call Chris, who picked up on the third ring. "Hello?"

"Chris? Hi, it's Abby Rawlings. I am so sorry about yesterday."

There was tension in Chris's voice, but I figured he was just still a bit miffed about yesterday. Part of me understood. I mean, Daddy did have business connections that he could have used. If anything, Daddy's construction teams needed at least one or two new trucks on almost a yearly basis, and if he made a good connection with me, he'd have an easy hundred thousand a year in fleet sales ready to go for Lake Automotive, never mind the actual construction itself with Chris's real estate investments. "Abby, it's good to hear from you. I was worried when you didn't show up yesterday. What can I do you for?"

I hated that turn of phrase, but I never let it show as I put my phone into the hands-free dock and started up my car. "Well, first off, I really wanted to apologize about yesterday. I was getting ready to go when Daddy kinda flipped out on me."

Chris's voice sounded relieved, and there was a chuckle in his reply. "Still a daddy's girl, I take it?"

"Forever and ever," I answered with a laugh. "Anyway, Chris, I was calling because of my friend, Shawnie. I saw in your texts that she made it to the party. I hope that wasn't a problem?"

"No, Shawnie was great," Chris answered. "I had a good time talking with her—she's quite a firecracker. Of course, it would have been nicer to have both of you beautiful ladies here at the same time, but I guess that'll happen another time."

"Maybe," I demurred, still not liking the weird undertone to his voice, "but I got a bit worried about her. She never came home last night, and she's not answering her phone. Do you know anything?"

"Hmmm, let me think," Chris said. "You know, she was hanging out with a few of the people at the party . . . you know, I can't remember their names. Let me check my—"

"What?" I asked, a tinge of panic creeping in.

"I was going to check my digital camera. I took a bunch of photos for the party, and I knew there were a few with your friend in them," Chris said. "But I think I left the camera at the lake house. If I had it, I'd remember who she was hanging out with."

"Chris, I know this is asking a lot, but do you think there's a way we could get that camera and take a look at the photos? Shawnie's not the sort of girl to go on a wild night without telling at least one person. I'd really appreciate it."

Chris hummed, and I thought he was about to say no, when the hum changed. "Okay. I'm a bit busy today, though, Abby. Do you mind if we just meet up at the lake house? I'm out that direction right now, and I can be there in a few minutes. And you could help me search for the camera. I think it's in the kitchen, but I'm not sure, and I don't have time to go around looking for it.

"Sure," I said. "That's more than fair."

"Okay. You know, Abby, I can pretty much figure out from your skipping out on the party that you're not really interested in seeing me again, at least not the way we used to be," Chris said. "But I'd like to think that we can at least be friends. We had some good times together."

"Yeah, we did," I answered, relieved. Maybe Chris had just sounded weird because he still carried a bit of a flame for me and didn't know how to say it. That could make anyone sound a little weird. "Thanks, Chris. I'll see you at the lake house. Can you send me a text with the address? That way I can put it into my GPS."

"Sure, I'll send it right away. It won't be hard to find, though. You shouldn't have a problem. See you in a bit."

Chris hung up, and my phone beeped a minute later as a new text message came in. I pulled over and read the text, copying the information over to my GPS system. A second later, I had my route, and I thought Chris was overestimating things a little bit. While the house wasn't exactly in the backwoods, the development was a decent distance from the other housing developments near the reservoir, and I wondered how long it would take for him to build all the infrastructure needed in order to get a good return on his company's investment.

167

Even if he only put in a two-lane drive, it was nearly a half-mile from the nearest blacktop.

Pulling back out into traffic, it took me about a half-hour to make my way to the house. The last mile or so was over a washboard dirt road, and I was somewhat worried about the suspension in my car as I drove. The Chevy Camaro is meant for city streets, not dirt paths. I slowed down, taking my time and ensuring I'd make it out to Chris's lake house.

Pulling up, I saw that the house was a boxy two-story affair, like it had been prepared by someone to use as a quick vacation getaway on the lake and not as a permanent or long-term sort of domicile. I saw a Jeep parked in front of the house, which I figured was Chris's, although the house did have a garage. "Probably where the old owners kept their boat," I said, looking at the way the driveway sloped all the way down to the lake. "That's where I'd keep it when I wasn't on the water, at least."

I parked next to Chris's Jeep, honked my horn and got out, waving when Chris appeared in the window. There was something about the way he looked, like he'd been surprised at my appearance. His face was a bit flushed, and a light sheen of sweat was visible on his forehead. "Hey, Abby!"

"Chris, thank you for meeting me," I said, walking toward the back porch. Chris came out, his face pink with an excited but naughty gleam in his eye. I swear it looked like I'd just walked in on him reading a porn mag and enjoying himself to it. "Are you okay?"

"A bit of a hangover, and I was looking around when you pulled up," he said, wiping his face before scrubbing his right hand on his shorts, blinking then letting out a big breath. "I didn't realize just how much of a big ol' mess we left yesterday."

Chris offered his hand and we shook hands. Chris moved like he wanted to give me a hug, but stopped about halfway, backing away a bit awkwardly. "Sorry."

"It's all right," I said, half apologetically. Even though he'd been the one to break it off with me, there were obviously lingering feelings. "So did you find the camera?"

"It's not in the kitchen, I can guarantee you that," he said, shrugging. "That was half the reason I was looking in the dining room. Unfortunately for me, there is a lot of junk there. Mind giving me a hand?"

"I guess not," I said, heading inside with him. I saw what he meant immediately, as the clear aftereffects of a good party were littered all around the place. "Sheesh, how many people did you have here yesterday?"

"Only about a dozen or so," Chris replied. "Not as big as some of the parties I threw back in my college days, but I'll admit I was pretty well buzzed by the end of the night. That's probably why I can't remember where I put my damn camera. Heck, part of me is a bit worried about what you'll find once we do find it."

"Sure it's not in the lake?" I teased, and Chris laughed.

"No, nobody brought any swimming gear, despite what I'd told you," Chris replied.

"Well, I'm just worried about my friend," I said, sighing. "I hope she's okay. There's just something that doesn't feel right."

Chris nodded and reached up, rubbing his temples. "I

understand. I'm sure she's fine though. Hey, you mind if I grab a drink?"

"I thought you were busy?" I asked, crossing my arms.

Chris waved me off with a relaxed laugh. "I am. I didn't mean alcohol. I just meant some fruit juice. There's still some orange juice in the fridge from last night. Would you like some?"

"Sure," I replied, trying to be polite. Besides, the day was warm, and I hadn't really had anything to eat or drink except for a mouthful of water when I'd quickly brushed my teeth. I could use it, and my grumbling stomach could use the calories. "If you have a big glass, that would be great."

"I'm sure I do," Chris said, heading into the kitchen area. He rooted around in the fridge for a moment, then came out with a glass pitcher of juice. "Here we are. I had to double-check that this wasn't one of the ones that are spiked."

Chris poured a large glass of orange juice, emptying the pitcher. "Oh. Well, there's some other stuff in there, and I think the carton of milk is calling my name right now. Here, go ahead."

I brought the glass to my lips, taking a deep drink. Chris watched me, smiling. His grin creeped me out, and I set the glass down. "What?"

"Nothing," Chris said, turning back to the fridge. He opened it up and took out a half-gallon jug of milk, breaking the seal. "Nothing at all."

## Chapter 14

### Dane

It was the best weekend I'd had in over five years, I thought as I lounged back on the couch. After getting home on Saturday night, I'd used the Internet to look at a few apartment listings online, and I was interested enough in two of them that I made plans to go see them on Sunday. The second complex was by appointment only, and while not great, it was pretty close to the Georgia Tech campus, had reasonable rent, included utilities and even a shared Wi-Fi connection that I could use. I booked an appointment to see one of their open units for Sunday afternoon, then went to bed.

Waking up, I enjoyed my morning workout and a shower before eating a light breakfast. As I ate, I pondered how best to talk with Chris about Abby. It shouldn't too much of a problem. After all, they'd been split for a while now, but still, there would probably be some weirdness that I wanted to minimize. Even if I was going to move out, Chris really helped me, and I didn't want to do him wrong. And frankly, bringing your friend's ex-girlfriend back to his place while you're crashing with him is just too weird—even for me.

When Abby first messaged me, I was a bit disappointed, but I understood. In the little bit of checking around I'd been able to do, Patrick Rawlings had struck me as the sort of guy who had gotten his success via a lot of hard work and a deep-seated stubborn streak that you didn't want to mess with. If even his own daughter had to sit back and think about the best way to approach him about our relationship, then I had to respect her point of view.

Besides, Abby constantly impressed me. Of course she was beautiful, as even the memory of us having sex on the side of the river, with the hum of the insects in the background, had caused my cock to stir lazily in my shorts. There was no need to do anything about it, though, as I knew that soon enough, Abby and I would be together again.

After lunch, I went over to the apartment and met the landlord. She was an Asian woman named Lynn, and when she looked over my application, she was reservedly impressed. "Well, Mr. Bell, it looks like you at least have a job," she said. "We get some folks in here who can't even claim that."

"Can I ask you, what percentage of your clients are students?" I asked, thinking that was what Lynn was talking about. "My girlfriend is going to do her Master's at Tech, and I was kind of hoping she might be able to crash here every once in a while."

"Not a lot of Tech students around here, but there are still quite a few students," Lynn answered with a shrug. "When I said no job, I meant nothing at all. The only way I take those folks is with two months' deposit up front in cash or money order. Then when their section eight comes in, I get our money. Still, sometimes it's not worth the hassle."

"And you don't have a problem with my background?" I asked incredulously. "No offense, just a lot of people have."

"Hey, you gotta stay somewhere," Lynn said. "I'll be honest with you, Mr. Bell. I'm not going to say you're going to make the wall of fame for this place. But I deal with some bad folks every week. If you pay your rent, don't destroy the place, and generally don't raise hell, I'll be happy. Then again, people like that rarely end up staying around here. They move on up and out."

We shook hands and I returned back to the apartment, stopping at a bookstore and picking up an interesting book. It was just a book on architecture, but it looked intriguing to me, and despite the rather hefty price tag of forty bucks, I didn't mind paying. I got home and decided that the best thing to do on such a relaxing day was just lounging on the couch. I sent Abby another text message and plopped down with my new book, intrigued almost immediately as I read about some of the great designers of the late twentieth century.

I was just reading about the background of Zaha Hadid when the door to the apartment opened and Chris came in. He was out of breath and sweating, but he looked happy, excited. In fact, I hadn't seen him this happy in a long time. "Hey, Dane! Great fuckin' day, ain't it?"

I realized what had gone on—Chris was drunk. I figured after the party he'd had Saturday, and with him not even coming home the night before, that he'd had enough. Apparently not, though, much to my disappointment. "Hey, Chris. Yeah, great day. What have you been up to?"

"Oh, this and that," Chris said with a laugh. He came in and took the chair opposite of the sofa, kicking his muddy shoes up onto the coffee table. "I see you got a new book. Good story?"

"Kinda," I said with a shrug. "It's a book on famous architects. So there isn't exactly a lot of plot to the thing. Still, the story about some of them, it is kinda interesting to see where they drew their ideas from, stuff like that."

"Sounds boring as shit," Chris dismissed with a laugh. "Tell you what, let me tell you a story instead. I promise—you're going to love it."

I knew that in this condition, Chris wasn't someone I wanted to fool with. Even drunk, I'd seen him fight three men and kick their asses like it was nothing, walking away without a scratch. While I could probably take him, I didn't want to hurt the one man that had given me a lifeline. Better to humor him, let him get it out of his system. Then I could look at maybe deflecting his attention somewhere else. Besides, getting into fights with my roommate was not the sort of person I wanted to be anymore. I set my book aside and sat up, paying attention. "Sure, go ahead, man."

"Well, it's about these two boys, so it's kind of a buddy-buddy story," Chris began, leaning back in the chair and crossing his hands over his stomach. "These two boys, oh, let's call them Tris and Boyd, they grew up together and raised a lot of hell together back in the day. Now, both Tris and Boyd were from well-to-do families, but deep down inside, both of them were disgusted by the boring nature of their lives. They tried the normal stuff that boys do, sports and games and toys and whatever, but life was just bleh and in tones of gray to them. It was only in each other that they were able to find some real fun."

I had a growing sense of disquiet as I listened to Chris talk. He was obviously talking about him and Lloyd, telling me about them growing up. There was something else he was trying to say, but I couldn't tell what yet. I decided it was best to listen carefully. "Go on."

"Well, starting in high school, Boyd and Tris found something that could at least partially relieve some of the tedious boredom that was their lives. That was sex. Now, before you start thinking anything, it wasn't with each other—they weren't into that. On the other hand, both of them absolutely had high interest in women. They developed this sort of game of one-upmanship, seeing who could score the greatest accomplishment. Oh, the two boys, they ran through the normal gamut. Boyd was the first to get a girl to give him a blowjob, Tris was the first to do some ass fucking, Boyd had the first threesome, stuff like that. By the time they were juniors in high school, they had reached a sense of boredom again. So, one day Tris said to Boyd, *we need to up the game*. Now, Boyd was an adventurous spirit, so he was more than willing. They started betting each other, seeing what the other one could pull off. At first, the bets were for real money, a hundred bucks or so, but soon enough, that same hundred-dollar bill had been passed back and forth so often that it became a symbol, a trophy more than an actual bet amount. The first challenge that Tris gave Boyd was to see who could screw their math teacher—a soon-to-be married young woman of twenty-four who'd just started teaching the year before and gave just about every boy in her class a nice set of blue balls along with his homework. Tris was able to bag that one, along with video proof, of course."

Chris grinned, and I was starting to feel sick to my stomach, not liking where this was headed.

"Even after Boyd had to move away, the two boys kept up their little game, emailing proof back and forth. Some of the proof ended up on the Internet, of course, but the boys were careful, making sure that their faces or voices were never identifiable in the videos. Some of the games were dangerous, but both of the boys eventually found a prize that they both enjoyed. That was in finding a woman or girl who at first would say no, then with some convincing, whether a little or a lot, would end up on her knees, begging for it. Then . . . well, then it went up a notch."

"Like how?" I asked, my throat dry and parched as I saw the true Chris. I'd seen him before, of course, but it'd been in firefights—in combat. I thought it was just the side of him that every soldier had. As Shakespeare wrote so much better than I could think of putting it,

In peace there's nothing so
becomes a man
As modest stillness and humility,
But when the blast of war blows
in our ears,
Then imitate the action of the
tiger:
Stiffen the sinews, summon up
the blood,
Disguise fair nature with hard-
favored rage,
Then lend the eye a terrible
aspect.

I knew that separation, and I thought that I'd only seen that in Chris and Lloyd in those times. Little did I know that the side I saw in combat was the real man, and the joking, easy-going guys I'd called friends were the false side of their natures. "What did you guys do?"

He seemed to ignore that I knew he was talking about him and Lloyd. "Oh, they started with alcohol, which is after all pretty easy to get their hands on and so effective more often than not. You see, Tris and Boyd were both handsome fellows. A lot of the early women, they didn't need much more than a little encouragement, something to help them let go of their inhibitions."

"Later on, with some of those women whose morals either refused alcohol or just couldn't be pried by other means, they got their hands on some of the little helpers that are so mislabeled in the media. A vial of this stuff in their drinks, whether it be water, beer, or even, say, *orange juice*, and the girl was out like a fucking light in about two minutes."

"Date-rape drugs? Fucking sick," I said, getting to my feet. "I don't know if this is just fiction or a true story, but I think I've heard enough, Chris."

"Oh, we're just getting to the best part, Dane. It's just getting good. You see, Tris and Boyd, they reunited when both of them joined the Army, although by then Boyd had picked up a battle buddy. Big, tall, handsome fucker, but dumb as a goddamned stump. Let's call him . . . Bane, why don't we? Anyway, Bane had the potential to be as much a player as Tris and Boyd—he certainly had the tools for it. Bane would have been a great player in the game, except for this little problem of his noble streak that ran bedrock deep in him. Tris and Boyd didn't mind, though. Bane was good in a fight, and like I said, he was as dumb as a rock. But reunited, the two friends were able to take their game to whole new levels. They'd finally reached the nearly penultimate level of their game, which they somewhat mourned, but knew it had been a shitload of fun anyway. You see, Tris and Boyd were both going to try and get a fresh, un-plucked cherry and turn her into a total mind-numbed slut. I mean, straight up ruin the bitch. Tris thought he had the edge. He'd found a total hottie who hadn't even graduated high school. She was stacked like a goddamned porn star, but as innocent and sweet as a Disney character. Nobody could have topped that, Tris was sure. He sweet-talked her, of course, pretending he was willing to wait for her. After all, this one would've sealed a victory. She was just about to give it up to him when the Army came calling, sending the boys to the big sandbox called Iraq. The thought of getting that precious cherry when he was back was what got him through it. Little did he know that Boyd had his own plans."

"You're a fucking psycho, Chris," I seethed, still not moving and not really understanding where this was going. Chris was nearly at his point, and his face twisted into a gleeful rage as he kept talking.

"Perhaps. Anyway, this one night, Tris thought he would play a trick on Boyd, so he slipped a quarter-vial of the assistance drug into Boyd's beer, just to knock him out. Maybe fuck with him a bit and make him think he'd shacked up with another man. He didn't realize that doing so would make Boyd drunk off his ass while still leaving him conscious and able to function. Tris found out later that not only had Boyd not gone back to the tent to sleep it off, but had in fact left camp, grabbing some local girl and hauling her back for a little fucking behind some supply tent. Now, you'd think that because the girl was saying no that it wouldn't count, but that didn't matter to the two boys. However, Boyd was stopped by Bane, who actually, get this, shot Boyd dead as a goddamned doornail. Total accident, of course, but Bane still went to jail for five years over it. Tris felt bad about the whole thing, so he decided to help his stupid ass buddy out. After all, Tris had given Boyd the quarter-vial, and Bane hadn't done anything more than defend himself. Anyway, during that time, Tris somewhat lost interest in the game for a while, and Miss Teen USA slipped away. Probably better in the long run, since it would protect him from any connection with the string of adventures the boys had. Little did he know that the girl would end up back in his life."

"Abby," I whispered, my fists clenching. Chris slapped his knee and sprang up, full of manic glee.

"Yep, that was her name! See, I just forgot, I guess. You must have heard this story before. Anyway, after Bane gets out, Tris sets him up, gets him a job, all of that. Then one day, he finds out from his uncle in passing that Bane stabs him in the back by fucking none other than Miss Teen USA! In fact, from what Tris could tell, Bane was probably fucking her three ways from Sunday! So Tris invited Abby to a fake party, hoping that he could get a little sugar through the right convincing. If anything, it'd kind of close out the game with a final score. But instead, Abby was so fucking love-struck that she sent her big-titted bitch friend in her place while she went off somewhere, probably fucking Bane and draining his balls of everything worthwhile. So, Tris got a little angry."

"What the fuck did you do?" I hissed, stepping forward. "And stop with this third person *Tris* shit." Chris brought his hands up, his eyes flashing with fire as he got to his feet, smirking as he dropped all the smoke screens and told the bare-faced truth.

"It's what I'm going to do that you should worry about. A vial to the friend, a vial to sweet Abby, and both of them are sleeping it off. When they wake up, they're going to find themselves in my nice, new little play room. Then it's going to be play time—all the time."

I couldn't resist it anymore. I swung. Unfortunately for me, I forgot the first rule of hand-to-hand combat as I was lost in my anger, which is don't let your emotions get the better of you. I should have kicked out straight, or thrown a jab. Instead, in my anger, I let loose with a huge, looping overhand right that Chris stepped inside of, catching my arm and attempting to judo throw me over his shoulder. I hung on, though, the two of us crashing to the floor in a tangle of bodies, arms and legs as I tried to pummel him. Curses and grunts filled the air.

Chris got a shot into my ribs as we rolled, a tight elbow that drove the wind out of me as I felt something inside me let go. Coughing, I hung on as best I could, trying to avoid the punches he began to rain down on my head and shoulders. While he punched, he was yelling. "Man, I so tried to get you into the game, to have some fucking fun. I figured if anything, prison would have made you more understanding. Instead, I come to find that you're fucking the one that I let get away? You probably even love the stupid stuck up cunt too."

"Fuck you!" I screamed, slipping my head to the side. Chris's punch, which had been aimed at my nose, slipped by, just clipping my ear before I could push the elbow up and over my head, allowing me to escape out the side. I wanted to try for a choke hold, but Chris was fast, scrambling to his feet and grabbing a small statue from the coffee table. He brandished it at me, the dull pewter-like metal gleaming in the afternoon light, suddenly deadly.

"Get out," Chris said, raising the statue up. I was on one knee, pain flaring through my body as my most likely separated rib sang out inside me. "Get out—you're on your fucking own. I tried, Dane. I gave you a place to stay, got you a job, I even took you out to get some pussy. But you just wouldn't go along with the program. So fuck you. You're on your goddamned own."

"I'll take this to the cops," I hissed, backing away slowly. "I'll call the cops, and I'll find Abby and Shawnie. You won't get away with this."

Chris laughed, breathless and with a trickle of blood running from the corner of his mouth. "You stupid fuck, you're even dumber than Lloyd. Who's going to believe you? The cops? You're a convicted killer, dipshit. You go to the cops, and you'll be the one arrested. Stalking, sexual assault, murder . . . oh, I'm sure they'd love to find everything. Because I bet if the cops did a rape kit on sweet, sweet Abby's corpse, they'd find your DNA, wouldn't they?"

I could see it in Chris's eyes; he would have a backup plan. It hit me like a ton of bricks. I'd been the fall guy. He knew that if he ever got into a jam, he could use me as a convenient excuse. After all, Chris was the upstanding member of society, from one of the best families that had served his nation honorably. I was just his fuck-up friend who he'd given a second chance to, the most noble of gestures that would be regretted sorrowfully.

"I will stop you," I gasped, backing away. I grabbed my phone from the counter as I approached the front door, glad that I still had my wallet in my pocket. "I don't know how, but I will."

"I don't think so, lover boy. By the time you figure things out, those two will be dead, and I'll be sitting here as free as a fucking bird. Get the fuck out. Next time I see you, I'm calling the cops myself."

Chris darted forward and shut the door in my face, throwing the lock. I knew from months in the apartment that the door was steel core, and the deadbolt could probably hold back a motivated gorilla if it needed to. I turned and limped as fast as I could toward the elevator, hoping that Chris's bragging had been in haste.

As the elevator descended, I tried to think of someone, something I could use to save Abby and Shawnie. Chris was right, the cops were useless. They'd believe him, and most likely *I'd* end up arrested. Instead, I had to find someone else. I racked my brain, trying to think. Hank? No, Hank Lake might have been a good man, but Chris was his family. I didn't really know anyone else at work well enough—I didn't even have anyone's phone number.

The bell to the lobby dinged at almost the same time that the answer came to my mind. *Daddy.* Patrick Rawlings might have wanted to shoot me, but he loved his daughter more than life itself or his dislike of me, warranted or not. If there was anyone in the world that could help me, and had the social influence to get the cops to believe him instead of Chris, it had to be Patrick Rawlings.

Of course, that left me with one major problem. Other than his name, I knew nothing of Patrick Rawlings, or even how to get in contact with him. I left the Mayfair Tower, then turned around. I walked into the concierge area, where the person on duty looked up at me in surprise. After all, I'd been living there for four months now, and other than snatching old newspapers, I'd never said a word to them. "Can I help you, sir?"

"Yeah," I said, trying to put as casual a look on my face as I could. Rule number one in a firefight: don't panic. If you panic, you're dead. "I'm trying to get a home phone number for someone. It's a business emergency, and nobody's at the office. Think you can help me out?"

## Chapter 15

### Abby

I felt consciousness come back slowly, achingly fighting its way back from the blackness that seemed to be smothering me. My mouth felt like it was lined in cotton, and my pulse pounded in my ears. I swore I could even feel the air resting against my skin, and everything was in pain.

I tried to move my arms to scratch the itch that had developed in my hip, and found that I was restrained somehow. I forced my eyes open, pain chasing away the last of my cobwebs as even the dim light of wherever I was sent stabbing needles through my eyeballs, directly into my brain. I mewled, trying to turn my head away.

"You're awake," someone said in a near whisper, which still sounded like I was at a rock concert. "I was getting worried."

I blinked, trying to get my eyes to focus. After a minute, I thought I could see a little bit, and recognized that I was in what looked like a garage, with a bit of dim light filtering through the one window that was in the corner. I guessed that it was nearly sundown, but that was all I knew. There was also a little light coming from what looked like maybe a twenty or forty-watt light bulb suspended from a socket in the middle of the room, but it cast more shadows than anything else.

I looked toward the voice that had spoken, and was shocked to see Shawnie trussed up, her clothes hanging in ripped rags from her body. "Shawnie? What the hell?"

"Don't worry, you look about the same way," she said softly, her voice dry and raspy. "Although I think I might be a bit more dehydrated."

"What happened? Where are we?" I asked again, still muddled. I looked up and saw that my hands were chained to a thick eye bolt in the beam that supported the ceiling. While the chains weren't super thick, and I wasn't exactly hung up like a side of beef, there was no way I was breaking that chain. It looked like the sort of chain you might use to hang a kid's swing or something, easily capable of supporting three or four times my body weight. "What the fuck?"

"We were drugged, we're in the lake house garage as best I can tell, and I have no fucking clue," Shawnie rasped, her voice gaining strength when she paused and forced herself to swallow whatever spit she could work up to lubricate her throat. "You certainly have interesting taste in men."

"Hey, I wasn't dating him anymore," I replied, wincing as my brain tried to kick off the rest of its cobwebs. "What happened to you?"

"I arrived at the house at the exact time that you told me," Shawnie said, rolling her shoulders. She was trussed up like I was, about six or seven feet away from me. I looked at her chains and guessed that if she stretched her arms overhead, she might be able to sit down, but that was it. Her clothes hung in tatters, and I felt a rush of shame as I noticed that I could see her left breast hanging out through a cut in her shirt, and that she was only wearing panties. I looked down and realized with a shock that I looked about the same way, although I was still wearing my shorts.

"When I got here, Chris was surprised as all hell, but he invited me in. He told me that he must have given you the wrong time, as the party wasn't supposed to start for another two hours. He seemed relaxed, and since it was hot as hell, when he offered me a drink, I accepted. Before you ask, no, it wasn't supposed to be alcoholic. I just asked for a glass of Coke. I was about halfway through my second cup when I started getting woozy, and it hit me. I woke up here this afternoon while he was chaining you up. What day is it, anyway?"

I blinked, tears coming to my eyes. "Shawnie, I'm so sorry. I didn't know that I was putting you in danger."

Shawnie shook her head and tried to wave it off with her fingers. "You didn't know, that's for sure. Can I ask, did you have any suspicion about this guy when you were dating?"

I shook my head, the pain lessening with each second. "No. But we didn't really spend a lot of time together. I mean, he was already in the Army when we started seeing each other. A lot of our courtship was done by phone calls, letters, emails, stuff like that. He was really sweet and charming at the time. He seemed like a normal guy when we were together though."

"So what day is it?" Shawnie asked, rasping. "I know it has to at least be Sunday, but I figure not Tuesday. I haven't had anything to drink, and while I'm pretty sure I pissed myself while I was out, I can't be sure."

"It's Sunday," I answered. I sagged, letting my head fall forward. "Shawnie, what are we going to do?"

She shook her head. "I don't know. Like I said, I've only been awake a bit longer than you. He must have dosed me a lot more. What brought you here?"

"I tried to text you last night, see how the party went. When I called Chris, he said that you were at the party, but that he didn't know who you'd left with. Where is your car, anyway?"

"I don't know," she said. Shawnie didn't drive her car often, it was a third-hand used thing that had a barely-working air conditioner, but it was all she had. "I drove it over here, but I heard Chris start up a car after he chained you up, driving off before he came back. I guess that was your Camaro?"

"Even drugged, I don't think you could confuse a beater Honda and a Camaro," I said with a mirthless chuckle. "I'm guessing he drove my car off to the same place that he took yours. Considering the area, that could be anywhere."

"It couldn't have been too far, he was gone only twenty minutes or so," Shawnie said. "I mean, I guessed it was twenty minutes. I can't see my watch very well. When he came back, he taunted me a bit, then left."

"What did he say?" I asked, chilled at the idea.

Shawnie shook her head, not wanting to relive the memory. Still, the information was important, she thought, and she swallowed thickly before continuing. "He didn't give a lot of details, but basically, he plans to rape us both and then kill us."

The calm, simple way she said it convinced me that Shawnie was pretty certain that she was going to die. I wasn't going out like that. I knew it for sure. Taking a deep breath, I screamed as loud as I could for help, until my breath was gone and a harsh, jagged pain racked my throat, like I'd swallowed a bone or something.

"Don't," Shawnie said when I stopped, forced to hack and cough to ease my vocal cords. "I already tried that. I stopped a while before you woke up."

"So what do you want to do?" I replied angrily. "Just stand here until it's time to be raped and killed?"

"I plan on surviving," Shawnie said simply. "I've just been trying to figure out what to do. Chris at least made a few mistakes."

"What's that?" I asked, getting my heart under control. It was hot in the garage, and while there was a trickle of cool air coming in from the currently open door to the rest of the house, sweat was beading on my forehead and trickling down between my breasts.

"The eye bolt isn't all that strong," Shawnie said, "and I don't think it's an actual full eye bolt. I think he used a U-shaped hook. If he can put it on there, it can come off too."

I looked up, moving around in the limited amount of space the chain's slack gave me. As I moved, I studied the beam above my head more closely, wondering if Shawnie was right. It was about six feet over my head, and from my angle, the shadows made it look solid, telling me nothing. Instead, I looked over at her bolt, and saw what she meant. What I'd originally taken to be a full circle was in fact a mostly closed U shape, like Chris had taken a hook and bent in the top. "Still, that looks like a pretty hefty hook. What's your plan?"

"Depends. How much do you weigh?" Shawnie asked. "Real weight, not Facebook weight."

"One fifteen, last time I checked," I said, thinking back to when I'd stepped on the scale. "I might be a bit heavier now. That was during the two-a-day spin classes."

"I'm one thirty-five," Shawnie said, "so I guess I get the painful one."

Before I could ask Shawnie what she meant, she looped the chain through her hands and dropped, jerking on the chain when her body came to a jarring halt an inch or so above the floor. She yelped in pain but got back to her feet. "What the hell are you doing?"

"Seeing if we can unbend the hook," she said before dropping again. The beam above her groaned but looked as strong as ever, and if there was any change to the hook itself, I couldn't tell. "I'm hoping that Chris knows more about cars and sexual torture than he does construction materials. And I'm hoping he's a cheap bastard."

"If the hook is soft enough, you might be able to get it to open some," I said, understanding her point of view. "But you might just jerk your arms out of socket at the same time."

"I'll take a surgery or two to avoid dying," Shawnie said, her breath coming fast and hard as she dropped again. Tears rolled down her face as she climbed slowly back to her feet, her head drooping. She shook her head, trying to repress the pain, and looked up at me, desperate for support, or at least a distraction. "Tell me something, Abby."

"What do you want to know?" I asked, looking up at her hook. Maybe there was a way I could do something instead of stand there like a damsel in distress, waiting for some hero to rescue me. I suck at that sort of thing—it doesn't fit my personality.

"Tell me about Dane," she said, taking a deep breath and tensing her forearms before dropping again. Blood trickled through her grip and down the chain looped around her left fist, and her face was a near mask of pain as she stood up. "Tell me that at least he was worth all of this damn trouble."

"I don't know if anyone is worth this shit," I said, trying to lighten the mood a little. "No, but really, beyond that Bad Boy exterior, he's got a good heart. We've really only had a few days together spaced out over nearly a month, but I really like him."

Shawnie stopped her dropping, looking at me in wonder. "Well, I hope something comes of it after all of this."

"He's not perfect, but he's perfect for me."

Shawnie grinned and flexed her hands painfully. "When is your and Mr. Perfect's wedding?"

"Well, let's not quite go there yet," I said, shaking my chains and looking up. "Hold on. You rest while I try something really, really stupid."

When I was a kid, I used to go to Gymboree after kindergarten. After Mom and my sister died, Daddy still had me going for a few years, at least until my body started to shoot up and he worried that I was getting too tall for becoming a gymnast. I'd tired of the class by then anyway, but I still did cheerleading in high school, although our squad was more of the dancer type than the gymnastics type. I had a pretty mean booty roll back in high school, if I do say so myself, although that didn't do much for my shoulder and back strength.

So it had been a few years since I tried anything like what I was about to do, but I figured there was no time like the present, and I couldn't think of any greater source of motivation, unless there were poisonous snakes or huge, ugly spiders in the garage as well that I wasn't seeing yet. The light through the window dimmed, and I thought the sun was nearly gone outside, night approaching. At least that would let some of the heat fade from the garage. That was something I could at least hope for.

I first tried my maneuver the strict way, grabbing the chain and pulling it tight enough to take away the slack. Chris had used a pair of handcuffs that he'd separated and then apparently welded to the main chain, so there was some pull on my wrists as I wrapped my hands through the chain and pulled up. The pain was immediate as the links tightened around the bones in my hand, and I gritted my teeth, trying to pull my feet up and to the chains. I was able to reach the cuffs, but the next phase of my plan fell apart as I couldn't get the strength to straighten out my legs and extend my body to the point of hanging upside down. Falling back, I gasped, flexing my aching hands. "Well, that version didn't work."

"Are you trying what I think you're trying?" Shawnie asked as she prepared herself mentally to drop again.

"I pulled it off when I was seven," I defended myself, sounding stupid even as it left my mouth. "It's worth a try."

Shawnie didn't have a reply, but dropped again instead, a scream tearing from her throat as she jerked to a stop. This time, she didn't get up so quickly, but pulled with her right arm only as she stood up. "Shawnie, what happened?"

"Left arm," Shawnie cried pitifully as she regained her feet. She tried but failed to stifle a sob, burying her mouth in her shoulder. "Maybe my elbow. It hurts, and I felt something pop in it."

"Then stop it," I said, looking up at the beam over my head. "I'll try to get us out of here. I'll try the cheat way this time. I should have the first time, except I'll be swinging like an idiot the whole time. Last time I did that on rings. I puked hanging upside down."

"I wouldn't, if I were you," Shawnie said. "Puke, that is."

"Thanks for the advice," I said, trying not to laugh despite the serious situation. I stepped back, and was just about to launch myself forward and up in the short amount of slack on my chain when the sound of a truck approaching came through to our ears. "Shit. Better hurry."

"No," Shawnie said sharply. "There's no way you can get that maneuver pulled off in time. Better to stay where you are. Maybe he gets stupid and we can kick him in the balls or something."

I stopped, nodding at the wisdom of Shawnie's words. "Okay, but promise me one thing."

"What's that?"

"Regardless of what happens, we fight this asshole until the end."

Shawnie clenched her fists and nodded. "Oh, you can guarantee that. Georgia boy's gonna learn what it's like to fuck with a Sandhills girl, that's for damn sure."

I heard the truck stop, and the door opened. Boots crunched on the dirt and gravel as someone approached. "You know, your accent gets stronger when you get angry," I commented, trying to calm the fear in my heart. "You really need to work on that."

"I love you too, Abby," Shawnie said, her smile disappearing as the back door to the house rattled and the heavy tread of the boots came inside.

"Honey, I'm home!" a slightly unhinged voice called, giggling crazily at the end. "And I've got such a surprise for you!"

I looked over at Shawnie, who nodded. We were going to fight, no matter what.

Chris came in, flipping on another light that momentarily blinded us before settling in and letting us see better. He'd had some sort of rough time, his shirt partially torn and a little crust of dried blood on the edge of his mouth. He had his right hand behind his back, and a gleam in his eye that sent chills down my spine. "Hey, baby, did you miss me?"

"Like I miss the bubonic plague," I spat back, literally, as I followed my words with the best loogie I could work up. Sadly enough, the garage was far too big and my spit was far too weak to reach the whole way across. It fell pitifully to the dust about two feet away from me, and I immediately regretted it as a waste of precious bodily fluids. "What the fuck do you want?"

"Well, I have some good news and bad news," Chris said as he crossed the garage. He stayed just out of my kicking range, even when I darted forward and tried to lash out at him. He laughed and jumped back, his hand still behind his back. "My, my, my, such fight in you still. That's not going to be useful at all."

"I don't plan on being useful to you, you sick, demented fuck," I hissed. Suddenly, Chris pulled his hand out from behind his back, holding what looked like a pistol. He pointed it at me for a second, then turned and fired. I screamed, sure that he had just killed Shawnie, but instead, the gun made a hissing, spitting noise and suddenly, Shawnie had a red dart sticking out of her left thigh.

"He shoots, he scores!" Chris taunted us both. Shawnie

stumbled back, her cry of pain fading as the drug in the dart took effect and she sagged down to her knees, unconscious. "Too bad. She's not going to be able to feel it. Ah well. You know, they say you should never eat chocolate before having your main meal, but in this instance, I'll break the rule."

"What the fuck are you going to do?" I asked as Chris walked toward Shawnie's body, squatting down and pulling the dart from her leg. "Get away from her, you psycho fuck!"

"Patience, my sweet. There's plenty of me to go around. But I want you to get a preview of what you're in store for, and I needed little Shawnie here to be . . . compliant."

I shook my chains and tried to kick him again, but he was still too far away. "What did you do to her?"

"Oh, nothing much. You see, I happen to have a rather fond interest in pharmaceuticals. It's what led me to making that little spike for your drinks, by the way, even though I got it on the Internet. Cheaper that way. But this baby," he said, holding up the red dart, "is my own special cocktail that I developed through a lot of experimentation. Little bit of Ecstasy, little bit of LSD, little bit of some other stuff . . . it's quite the ride, I've heard. Fact is, if I shot you up with this, Abby, I could fuck you three ways from Sunday, and not only would you not remember it, but during the whole thing, you'd be begging me for more and more. Too bad you two won't be getting a repeat performance though. Your boyfriend ensured that."

"What?"

Chris turned and threw the dart at me, bouncing it off my chest. His voice broke into a high-pitched, wheezy scream, the last vestiges of his sanity disappearing as his voice jumped an octave. "Knowing that stupid noble fuck, he's probably trying to convince the cops right now that I'm doing what I'm doing. So, I can't have any evidence left behind. Damn shame, though, what'll happen tonight afterward. Two young women, so close to graduation and chasing their dreams, decide to go camping up in the Chattahoochee National Forest. Of course, being unprepared, they both disappear, only to be found later badly decomposed near Blue Ridge Lake."

"You're a monster," I gasped. "A real monster."

"You have no idea," Chris said with a chuckle. "But at least I'm honest about it. I know I'm a monster and relish the fact. Now, the monster must prepare for his first lesson."

Chris turned and walked back into the rest of the house, humming to himself as he went.

I started to pray. First to God, and then I took something from Dane's Book. In a last gasp of desperation, I said a quick one to Odin. Maybe the Norse deities could bring Dane to me. Something or someone had to—I was all out of ideas.

## Chapter 16

### Dane

My heart was in my throat as I got out of the taxi, giving the driver twenty bucks. "Keep the change," I told him. "Thanks."

"Hey, no problem, man. It ain't my business, buddy, but you want me to wait? You don't look like you're expecting to be received too well."

"No, I'm good," I answered, waving him off. "One way or another, I'm not leaving for a while."

"Your choice," the driver said, looking around. I could understand his concern. I looked like shit, with a half-torn shirt, my hair all messed up, and a mouse growing under my left eye. Still, I wouldn't be stopped.

Smoothing my hair back as best I could, I for the first time wished I'd kept the short hair I'd had in the military. At least that way, I wouldn't look like a total lunatic.

Approaching the door, I squared my shoulders and rang the front doorbell. There was a long chunk of silence, and I reached for the doorbell again when I heard steps coming toward the door. "Coming!"

The door rattled, locks being thrown back before opening, and I saw a woman standing in the doorway. She was about forty-five, or maybe a well put together fifty, with a certain coldness to her features that told me that she was from upper crust society. I guessed I had just met Brittany, Abby's stepmother.

I cleared my throat and spoke in my most polite voice, regardless of the hurricane of emotions roaring through me. "Mrs. Rawlings, I need to speak to your husband. It's very important."

Her look told me everything I needed to know. I'd seen it over two hundred times before, applying for jobs before starting at Lake Ford. It was the look that said *fuck off.* "I'm sorry, but Patrick is not available right now. I suggest trying him at the office on Monday."

She closed the door in my face, but before she could lock it, I stepped back and kicked as hard as I could. I wished I had on my work boots, but the running shoes were enough to do the trick, and the door flew back, Mrs. Rawlings tumbling to the floor from the force. "Can't wait," I said, stepping over her and walking inside. "I'm sorry."

"Brittany?" a man called from the back, followed by the sound of rushing feet. "What the hell was that?"

Patrick Rawlings came around the corner into the main hallway, stopping dead in his tracks. "You."

"Me," I said, dismissing the venom in his voice. I couldn't deal with his bullshit right now. I needed his help. If he wanted to hate me after that, I wouldn't stop him. "We need to talk."

"I'm calling the cops," he said, stepping back and heading down the hallway. "Your ass is going back to jail."

"Fine, call the cops, but tell them to rescue Abby first!" I yelled after him. "She's in trouble, and I need your help!"

Patrick's footsteps stopped, and I heard Brittany start to get up off the floor. I waited for Patrick to return, and in the meantime I held out my hand to Brittany, offering her assistance up off the floor. "Sorry about that. I just couldn't waste any more time."

197

She didn't respond, but took my hand and let me help her up. "I need your help," I repeated to her instead.

"You said that already," Patrick replied as he came back into the room. "Tell me what you mean."

I wasn't sure where to begin, so I started from the day before. "Yesterday, Abby and I spent the day together," I started, pausing when I saw the expression on her father's face. I'd mentally punched him in the gut, or maybe a few inches higher, right in the heart, but I couldn't afford the pity right then. "She knew you'd object, so she told you that she was invited to a party."

"Yes, with Chris Lake," Patrick said. "They used to date, back when she was in high school."

"I know. To try and make up for it, Abby asked her friend, Shawnie, to go in her place, with an excuse and apology. This morning, she was supposed to tell you the truth."

He crossed his arms over his chest, nodding. "When she found me this morning, she said that her friend hadn't replied to a text message, and she just wanted to check to see if she was okay."

"I got a text saying that she had to do something," I said. "We exchanged a few more messages, the last a bit after noon. Then, about an hour ago, Chris came home to the apartment. Mr. Rawlings, I know this is crazy, but Chris kidnapped both girls. He plans to drug them, and I think . . . well, I don't want to say it."

"How do you know?" Brittany asked. "How can we trust you?"

"Does this look like a fucking joke?" I hissed, pointing to my eye. I pulled up my t-shirt, showing her my already bruising rib. "What about this? That fucking psycho has Abby and Shawnie, and you're doubting my word?"

I was angry, breathing hard and trying not to scream at her. Patrick watched it all, then nodded. "Fine. I'll believe you. What do you need?"

"Abby said the party was out by the reservoir. What did she mean?"

He nodded again. "Blalock Reservoir. She said that Chris had signed a big real estate deal out there. At least half of the shoreline is undeveloped."

"That must be it," I said. "I need you to get the cops out there, somehow. I couldn't go to them—that's why I came here. Tell them whatever you want, but you have to get them out there. They won't believe me. I'm a fucking felon with a dishonorable discharge to my name. Even you hate me. But I swear by everything I hold dear in this world, I am telling the truth."

"Okay," Patrick said without a second's hesitation. He turned around and went to the back, returning a moment later with his phone and the keys.

"You drive," he said, tossing me the keys. "I'll talk to the cops and the phone company while you drive. Follow my directions. I know where the reservoir is. Brittany, you stay here in case we're on a wild goose chase. I pray that we are."

"Be safe, Patrick," Brittany called. "And get her back. I love you."

He stopped in the doorway, turning to his wife. "I love you too, sweetheart. Don't worry. If this is true, we'll get her back."

His vehicle was a heavy duty Chevy Pickup, complete with off-road tires. I felt about twenty feet tall sitting in the driver's seat, and a small part of my mind flashed back to the time I'd driven an armored Humvee on patrol in Iraq. It was about the same size.

Patrick mistook my momentary flashback for a question about his choice of vehicle. "I have another, but this should be better for our needs," he said, sliding into the shotgun seat. "Think you can handle it?"

"Quite," I said, starting the engine and putting it in drive. I jammed the accelerator to the floor, heading out toward the main street. Old habits die hard, and while it had been five years, I could still drive well. "Where do we go?"

"South, along 75," Patrick said. "I think the exit is 224. It's the Hudson Bridge Road exit."

"Gotcha," I said, gaining speed. A terrible dread settled in my stomach as I pushed the truck past sixty, shooting through a red light and earning a few honked horns. "Hope your insurance is paid up."

Patrick didn't reply, instead calling the cops. He talked with the dispatcher for a few minutes, explaining the situation. When he hung up, he was pissed off. "Fucking cops can't do much without knowing an address," he said. "And Abby has only been missing a few hours. Shit!"

"Calm down," I replied, my fingers tight on the wheel. "Abby told me you've had heart problems in the past. I don't need you having a fucking coronary on me while trying to help Abby."

Patrick glanced at me, then shook his head. "What is it with you, Bell? You kill your friend, but now you're trying to save my daughter?"

"I killed my friend because he was trying to rape a teenage Iraqi girl, and he was going to stab me with a bayonet," I answered, not taking my eyes off the road as I shot up the on-ramp to the Interstate, already going seventy-five. "As for Abs, she's a special girl, as I'm sure you know."

"Yeah, I do," Patrick replied. "Hold on, let me try something. I gave Abby a Camaro as a graduation gift from high school."

"Yeah, I rode in it yesterday. Nice car. You got it tuned up, too."

Patrick grunted in acknowledgment, then continued. "I had it equipped with OnStar. Her phone is under my contract, and that damn gadget has every gizmo on the planet on it."

I saw where he was going. "You can have those tracked. The car's OnStar and her phone's GPS. One of them should still be working."

"That's what I figure," Patrick replied. He dialed his phone again, talking to an OnStar rep. As the official owner of the car, he was able to get the car's location and have it sent to his truck, where it popped up on an in-dash navigation system. "Finally, a use for that hunk of junk. Abby insisted I get it though. Never have used it for more than a fancy clock and CD player until now."

"More importantly, now you can tell the cops," I added, watching as the route to the point was laid out over the navigation.

He shook his head. "OnStar is doing that for me right now. They can feed the cops the exact GPS coordinates. I'm going to try and get an aerial shot of the area though, just in case."

He tapped at his phone, cursing occasionally as he fiddled with the unfamiliar technology. "After this, remind me to learn how to use this goddamn thing," he finally said. "I just let Abby do most of this for me."

"I will," I replied, pushing the truck faster. Above ninety, it started to shimmy some. The high tires and boxy exterior were meant for rugged low speeds and not aerodynamics, so I kept the speed down at eighty-five. "Four miles until the exit."

"Do you love her?" Patrick asked randomly, his head still buried in his phone. "You're not just trying to seduce her?"

"I'll die for her if I need to," I answered grimly. "I came to your door—hell, I kicked it down, knowing there was a decent chance I'd end up catching a shotgun to the chest. Does that answer your question?"

"I think it does," Patrick replied. "I knew you two were still talking, by the way."

"How?" I asked.

He pointed to his phone. "I get a detailed bill on the phones by email every second of the month. That includes every number that she's called or texted in the past thirty days."

"She was angry with me when she found out who I was. I wasn't trying to mislead her, but that first night, I didn't really know who she was either."

I got off the Interstate and kept following the navigation. I knew at some point soon I'd have to keep my eyes open. The way Abby had described the house, the road likely wasn't going to be well-marked or even paved.

Patrick looked out the window, seemingly lost in thought before he spoke up. "After her mother and sister were killed, I only had Abby," he said softly, looking out on the rapidly dimming evening sky.

"If I was overprotective, it was because I couldn't stand to lose her too."

"You won't," I promised, turning right. "I think this is the right road. I see a house up ahead—see the lights?"

"No," Patrick admitted. "You must have better eyes than me."

The road quickly became rough and bumpy, and I wondered if we were on the right track. Still, the house grew closer and closer, and we were getting closer to Abby's car, too. I gunned the engine, not caring if we tore up the shocks on the truck. Patrick said nothing, putting his hand on the dash and hanging on grimly while we bounced our way down the washboard road.

The house was on the edge of the lake, a two-story job that looked like it wasn't quite good enough to be a permanent house, but had when it was originally built been a pretty good vacation getaway. On our left, I could see blue lights approaching, and I knew the cops were approaching on another road, probably one that ran along the edge of the lake. Still, they were a good distance away and weren't rushing the way we were. I couldn't trust that they'd get there in time, and I pushed the engine harder.

I skidded to a halt in front of the house, still a quarter-mile from the readout for Abby's car. Still, the house was the best chance for her location, and I was desperate, spraying gravel from the tires and leaping out. I immediately heard a sound that made my blood run ice cold, as Abby screamed as loud as she could. Running, I headed for the back of the house where I heard the sound coming from. It sounded like the garage, but there was no visible front door, with the garage door itself firmly padlocked shut. I went around and up the short stairs to the back porch, finding the rear entrance. This time, instead of kicking, I lowered my shoulder, hitting the door like I did back when I was on the high school football team. The old frame nearly exploded as I bulled through, looking for someone or something to fight. There was an open door leading down to the garage, and then a sound that again sent chills down my spine, as Abby's scream was cut off like a switch with a harsh, slapping sound. "Shut up, bitch."

Ironically, what should have driven me to even greater levels of rage, instead pushed me all the way past my emotions, drawing me into the cold, calculated place that I had last touched nearly five and a half years ago in Iraq. The killer inside me, the one that had actually shot at people with intent—and been rewarded, not sent to jail—was loose, and glad to be out of his mental cell. Almost unconsciously, I reached out and scooped up a kitchen chair, brandishing the wooden legs in front of me like a lion tamer as I jumped the short three steps down to the floor.

The first thing I saw was Abby, trussed up and bound like a side of beef, her arms cinched above her head and her eyes half-shut, bruised and battered but still conscious, if only barely. She was alive at least, and I had to secure the area, so I turned my eyes away, scanning the rest of the room.

The next thing I saw was Chris, a knife in his hand, brandishing it toward me. Next to him, sagging in her bonds and moaning, was Shawnie, who'd been cut numerous times, the blood dark on her skin in the overhead fluorescent light.

"One more step, and I cut her fucking throat," Chris said, quickly stepping behind Shawnie and pulling her hair, exposing her neck. "Don't think I won't do it, hero boy."

"Drop the knife, Chris," I said, lowering the chair. It wasn't an effective weapon anyway. I had used it just to shield myself as I came through the door. My killer side knew that right now, the best thing to do was to get him to talk. Killing could come later. "The cops are right behind me, and you don't want a murder rap on top of it all. Trust me, I know."

Chris chuckled and pulled Shawnie's hair harder. She was obviously drugged, her eyes rolling in her head. Somewhere, deep down, I think she knew what was going on. "Don't think I can get any worse than this, Dane, my boy. Two kidnappings, assault, and of course, the testimonies you and Abby there will give against me? No way, that's not looking too good at all."

"You let them go, I let you go," I said simply. "On my honor."

Chris's knife faltered, and he looked at me in slight distrust. "Why would I trust you?"

I shrugged and sat down on the chair, even though it took everything in my power to do it. "You trusted me, gave me a place to stay. You could have turned me out, let me fucking hang. You didn't. I owe you my life. I think this makes us even."

Chris's knife faltered, drawing away from Shawnie's throat, which is what I wanted. What I didn't plan on, however, was Shawnie. Seemingly trapped in a drug-induced state, she threw her head back, her skull smashing into Chris's nose and mouth, sending him stumbling backward into the wall.

I was out of the chair and on him in a flash. Driving low, I hit him hard with my shoulder in his stomach, lifting him and bouncing him again off the side of the garage. The knife fell from his hand to clatter on the ground, out of his grasp and temporarily out of my concern.

Not giving him a chance to recover, I threw him to the side, bouncing his body off the floor before nailing him under the chin, snapping his head up and back with a kick that would have put a football through the uprights at a good distance. I stood over him, trembling while the killer inside me warred against the better half of my nature, until finally a compromise was reached.

"Never trust a convicted killer." I spat at the unconscious body. I kicked him as hard as I could in the ribs, feeling something give way under my foot with a satisfying crunch. "Sick fuck."

I heard a whimper behind me and I turned, seeing Shawnie's desperate and half-lidded, drugged out eyes. "Sorry, Shawnie. I'll try and be gentle."

I stood up and looked at the bonds Shawnie was being held with, trying to figure out what to do, when I heard a choked gasp behind me. "Abby?"

Patrick's body hit the floor before I could even get to him, his hands clutching at the left side of his chest. His face was paper white, except for two bright red blotches on his cheeks. He looked like a porcelain doll in a perverse way. "Heart . . ."

"Don't you fucking die on me," I growled, pulling him up and out of the garage and back into the kitchen. I lifted his feet up and grabbed the other kitchen chair, elevating his legs and hopefully helping his heart. You're supposed to do it for shock, but I had to do something. "Hold on, the cops will be here in a second."

I could hear the car approaching, far too slow for my taste. "Move it, you fucking Deputy Dawgs!" I screamed before loosening Patrick's clothing. "I can't do all this shit by myself!"

"Abby?" Patrick whispered, reaching up and taking my hand. I squeezed his fingers, staying next to him. "Where's Abby?"

"She's fine," I said, lying through my teeth. I had no fucking clue how Abby was, except that she was alive. "I don't think Chris touched her."

"I'm sorry," he whispered, his eyes fluttering shut. His head sagged back, and I leaned down, checking him. No heartbeat.

"Shit!" I grunted, tearing open his shirt to double check. "Don't you fucking die on me, old man!"

I heard Abby stirring in the garage, just as the cop car stopped outside. The doors to the car closed, and I heard the scrape of boots on the dirt. "Move your asses, boys!" I yelled even as I interlaced my hands and looked for the compression point. It'd been years, but the basics of giving CPR were still there in my mind. "I've got a man in cardiac arrest in here!"

## Chapter 17

### Abby

I came to slowly, groggy from the slap Chris had hit me with. When I did, the first thing I noticed was that I was lying on the ground with a woman kneeling above me. "Miss Rawlings?"

"Who are you?" I muttered, blinking. The light was now dim, but I had a pounding headache. "Where is Shawnie?"

"Your friend is being looked after," the woman replied. "I'm Debbie Morgan. I'm a cop."

"What happened?" I asked, rubbing my head.

"Mr. Lake has been arrested. He's in an ambulance as well," the cop said. She helped me sit up, making sure I kept my head down and between my knees. I noticed that I'd been covered with a blanket, which helped explain why I was so warm. "Your friend and your father are also on the way to the hospital."

"Daddy?" I asked, jerking my head up and sending a lightning bolt of pain through my head. "Is he all right?"

"Your father was taken to the hospital with chest pains," the cop replied. "We're going to take you there as soon as a car gets here. We had to get the others out of here first."

"Dane?" I asked. "I heard him before Chris knocked me out."

"Mr. Bell?" The cop asked, then pointed. "He's been arrested too. We'll make sure he won't hurt you again."

I shook my head, struggling to get to my feet. When the cop tried to restrain me, I pushed her hands away. "Let go of me! Dane didn't do anything. He's my boyfriend. He was trying to save me."

The cop stopped, looking in my eyes. I rolled my eyes, despite how much it hurt, and got up. "I'm not loopy, and I'm not on drugs. Dane is my boyfriend, and if he's here, it's because he saved us."

"That's what I keep telling them," I heard Dane say from the other room, grunting when someone shoved him. "Just nobody believes me."

"Shut up, traitor," someone in the other room grunted, and I heard a loud smack and the thud of a body hitting the floor. The cops around here weren't exactly the most understanding nor the most likely to follow the rules in terms of use of force, especially against convicted felons.

"Stop it!" I yelled, wincing at the pain in my head as I made my way into the other room, which turned out to be the kitchen. Dane was lying on his side, his hands cuffed behind his back while his eyes stared holes into a cop who was standing over him. "I'm telling you, he wasn't involved! What's your name? I'm going to sue your ass!"

The cop looked at me, surprise registering in his face for the first time before turning and walking away. I looked at the other two cops in the room, who both looked sheepish at the ferocity in my voice. One of them, the cop who'd helped me wake up, went over and helped Dane to his feet. "Okay, I'm going to go by her word," she said softly to Dane. "On the promise that you don't go anywhere. We'll ride over to the hospital together. How's that sound?"

"I'm good," Dane said, shrugging off the cop's arm and sitting back down in the chair. "And tell your buddy out there he's lucky that I'm more forgiving than Abs is."

The cop nodded and stepped back, gathering her fellow cops and leaving us alone. "Are you okay?" Dane asked as soon as we had a bit of privacy. There was still a cop in the room, but we lowered our voices. I wanted to reach out to Dane, but at the same time, I knew if I did, the cops would get interested again. "Are you hurt?"

"I should probably get checked for a concussion," I replied, "but if you mean am I in the same boat as Shawnie, no."

The female cop came up to us again, this time looking less concerned. "Miss Rawlings? We have an ambulance coming to take you to the hospital."

"And Dane?" I asked. "Can he come along with me?"

She looked at us, then nodded. "Yeah, we can do that. Come on. Mrs. Rawlings is supposed to already be at the hospital."

\* \* \*

One of the nice parts about living in a city like Atlanta is that there are a lot of top-flight hospitals throughout the city. When the ambulance pulled up, I'd already been checked out by the paramedic, who confirmed that while my clothes had been torn, Chris hadn't done anything else. "You've probably got a low-grade concussion," he advised me before we pulled up, "but I'd let the docs give you a full check out. No offense—I don't know if you need it or not, but you've got one hell of a civil lawsuit on your hands."

"Not my style, but I'll still let the doctor look," I said, not mentioning the fact that Daddy had enough money that he didn't need to worry about the frivolity of a civil suit. "Do you know anything about Shawnie or my dad?"

The medic shook his head, and the ambulance stopped. Dane,

who had been allowed to ride in the front seat next to the driver—the cops still weren't trusting him—called back. "We're here."

I found Brittany immediately inside the emergency room, the paramedics still insisting that I ride on the gurney. "Come off it, guys, I can walk," I complained, pushing them away. Brittany put her hands on my shoulders, pushing me back. "Brittany . . . Daddy?"

"They have him upstairs," Brittany said, trying to maintain a calm outer demeanor. Still, I'd known her long enough; her emotions were a total wreck. "Abby, how did it all happen?"

I told her the story while we waited for the doctor. The whole time, Dane didn't leave my side, reaching out and taking my hand and holding it gently. "It's my fault, Mrs. Rawlings," Dane said softly. "I should have seen what was wrong with Chris before all of this happened."

"You weren't the one who lied and tried to get Shawnie to cover for you," I said, tears coming to my eyes. "This is all my fault."

I'd expected anger from Brittany, or at least derision. Instead, she leaned down and hugged me, then hugged Dane. "It is neither of your faults. Neither of you truly knew what kind of man he was. I remember him from five years ago, and he seemed like a normal, fine young man then."

"Regardless of whatever else you've done in your life, know that you redeemed yourself with what you did today," I added.

"I agree," Brittany added. "The ambulance driver told me when they brought Patrick in that you most likely saved his life."

"What do you mean?" I asked, confused. "What did you do?"

"I attempted CPR," Dane said simply. "It was only for a minute or two until the cops got there and took over."

"Don't forget the thirty seconds you continued even after they pulled their pistols on you," Brittany said.

I gaped at Dane for a moment, then shook my head. "That would be like you. No wonder the cops were pissed at you after I woke up."

"So how is he?" Dane asked, "And Shawnie?"

"I don't know about the girl," Brittany said, "but they took Patrick upstairs. The doctors looked . . . not too worried. I don't know if that's a good sign or a bad one, but I'm praying for the best."

Just then, a doctor approached me, a professional smile on his face. "Miss Rawlings? I'm Doctor Jones. I just got done talking to the paramedics who brought you in, and I thought I should come over here and see how you're doing."

"Can Brittany and Dane stay?" I asked, leaning back on the gurney. "And can I at least get up?"

Dr. Jones looked around, then nodded. "Just stay back, if you could. I don't think this should take too long."

"Don't worry, I'll be right outside the curtain," Brittany said. "I've seen the inside of those exam areas. They're tiny."

Dr. Jones had a nurse wheel my gurney to an exam room, where the bed was at least reclined rather than flat. "Okay, just look into the light . . . pupils look good, pulse is good . . . any pain?"

"Some, but mostly in my jaw where he caught me," I said. "I'm not going to be eating meat any time soon."

Jones nodded and touched my jaw gently, humming when I winced. "You've got a pretty good bruise forming there. All right, as a precaution, I'm going to order an x-ray. Also, I'm going to admit you overnight, mainly to see if you've got any side effects of whatever it was that you drank that knocked you out."

"Doc? What about Daddy?" I asked, worried.

"I'll go check. If you can talk, I doubt your jaw is broken, but your dentist would probably feel better if I did it anyway. The nurse should be by soon in order to get your information and take you up to get an X-ray."

The doctor left, leaving me and Dane alone. I could hear Brittany shuffling back and forth outside the curtain, but I took the moment to enjoy it with Dane. "Thank you. I know I was only out a few minutes, but you saved my life."

"You saved mine," Dane said. "You renewed my purpose in life."

We held hands for a few minutes, just looking at each other, and despite the background noise of an emergency room, I felt peace dropping over me, soothing the panic that was gnawing at my mind about Daddy and his health. I heard the curtain pull back, and I turned, hoping it was the doctor. Instead, it was Brittany, who was looking at me in a way she never had before. It was like she finally had recognized me for being an adult, and not just a child. "If you need anything, just let me know, and I'll make it happen," she said simply. "I'm sorry, Abby."

"It's okay, Brittany. Let's wait for Dr. Jones and see what is going on with Daddy."

"Actually, I do have a request," Dane asked, a bit sheepish. "The cops took my wallet, and I'm kind of homeless right now. Can I borrow fifty bucks for the night?"

"Dane, you can stay at the house," Brittany immediately said. "You saved my husband's life and Abby's life. I'm quite sure that deserves a decent bed and a hot meal once we get out of here."

A man in a dark suit walked up, flashing a badge. "I'm sorry, Mrs. Rawlings. That might be a while. I'm Agent Morgan of the Atlanta FBI. I'd like to talk to your stepdaughter about her kidnapping."

Doctor Jones came back, tapping his pen on a clipboard. "Not for at least twelve hours, Agent Morgan. Testing and observation. In the meantime, though, a bit of good news. Mr. Rawlings is going to be just fine. Mr. Bell's quick thinking turned what could have been a major, if not fatal, heart attack into a minor incident. He'll be here for a few days, but according to the guys I talked to in the cardiac unit, he should make a full recovery."

I nodded, smiling for the first time in what felt like forever. "Then let's get my X-rays done too. After that, regardless of what you say, Doc, I'll be happy to talk to the cops. That piece of shit needs to pay."

* * *

The FBI agents who accompanied Agent Morgan the next morning were your pretty typical group. One of them, who introduced himself as Agent Jacobi, came straight from FBI central casting. White, nondescript, but with an intensity to his eyes that spoke of his dedication to his work. I saw a plain gold wedding band on his finger, but there was something about it that made me think it was mostly there for show. He was married to the Bureau, not to any other person.

The other one, Agent Leeds, was a woman in her mid-thirties, and from the first time she opened her mouth, I could identify her for what she was—a lab geek. As a biology major, I've dealt with plenty of them in my studies. They're generally a good group of people, but they normally have social skills that are a little lacking. The little pink streak in her hair gave it away.

Agent Jacobi opened up the questioning. He asked me about my history with Chris Lake, including our dating history. "So you never had intimate relations with him?" he asked, all business. "Just to be clear."

"Never," I said clearly. "Previously, we went to second base, but never any further."

Jacobi made a note in his notebook, while Leeds tapped at her tablet. I assumed she was recording the whole conversation using the computer. She had arranged it very specifically to point the back toward me. Besides, it struck me as just fitting her personality.

We moved on to the actual details behind Shawnie's and my kidnappings, Jacobi asking a few questions related to the symptoms that I felt. "No, I didn't notice any sort of taste about the juice at all. It just tasted like normal orange juice."

"And how fast did it take to kick in?" Leeds asked, the first time she had said anything since they had introduced themselves.

"I'm not sure, but I'd say fewer than five minutes," I said. "I don't think I even finished the glass."

Agent Leeds put her finger to her lips, nodding thoughtfully. I jumped at the chance. "Can you guys tell me what I was dosed with?"

Leeds shook her head. "Right now, we're not too sure. The problem is that your blood tests all came back pretty clear. Whatever it was, it gets filtered out very quickly."

"Have you searched his apartment?" I asked, feeling dumb as soon as I did. Of course they had. They were the FBI.

"And his office," Agent Morgan said. "Miss Rawlings, you're probably wondering why this is being handled by the FBI and not the Atlanta Police."

"Not really," I said. "Daddy is a fan of those procedural cop shows, and I know that while they're normally full of junk, there's some information that jives. I'm guessing you have investigations over multiple states?"

Morgan nodded, impressed. "Good catch. That, and the kidnapping gives us the ability to take the lead on this. Miss Rawlings, I'm not going to lie. We suspect Mr. Lake in a series of sexual assaults stretching back at least five years. If the statement Mr. Bell gave us holds water, it may even go back further, although the ones before the use of any drug would be nearly impossible to prove. You're quite lucky, Miss Rawlings."

"Why?" I asked, a chill sweeping over me as I thought about all those victims, all those women who'd been seduced or assaulted by Chris for his sick game with Lloyd.

"Because a pattern was emerging in our investigations," Leeds said, geeking out and not realizing how fast her mouth was running away from her. "We think he was getting ready to graduate from taking his thrill from sex to murder."

I shivered, hugging my knees, and Leeds realized what she'd said. "Sorry," she muttered, looking around sheepishly. "I shouldn't have said that."

I shook my head, looking down. "It's okay. Tell me, is Shawnie okay?"

"She's going to need a little more recovery time, but she'll be okay," Agent Jacobi said simply. "Mostly uninjured, but there are a lot of superficial cuts and a separated shoulder from her escape attempt."

I nodded. "Then how about we wrap this up, and let me go see my friend and hopefully my dad?"

It was Agent Morgan's turn to look sheepish, and he ran a hand through his thinning brown hair. "Actually, Miss Rawlings, you might need to wait for your clothes. Uhm, unless you mind wearing a pair of scrubs or something. I'm sure your stepmother or Mr. Bell will bring a pair as soon as they're done."

"Where are they, anyway?" I asked. It was already mid-morning, and I had thought they'd already have been at the hospital. "With Daddy?"

Agent Jacobi shook his head. "No, wrapping up things with Atlanta PD," he said. "I believe there is a little situation of someone putting cuffs on Mr. Bell that needs to be cleared up. Also, they'll take another statement from him, although we talked with him last night. His story and yours are pretty clear. It all matches what your friend said as well."

"Then let me get some scrubs, and I'll go see Shawnie. Is there anything else you need?"

Agent Morgan looked at his coworkers and shook his head. "We might be in touch soon. For sure, the prosecutor will want you to be available to testify, but that might be a long time off."

"That's fine. Right now, I want to see three people: Daddy,

217

Shawnie, and Dane. In that order."

## Chapter 18

### Dane

The doctors were actually super conservative with both Shawnie and Patrick, keeping both of them in the hospital for over a week. I kept myself busy during that time, going into Lake Ford two days after the attack to clean out my locker. As soon as I walked in, I could feel the uncomfortable silence from everyone. Chris's arrest had made not just local but national news, and most of the details that could be released already had been. Of course, the effect on Lake Automotive was immediate and crippling. The lot was as empty as a ghost town, and the repair shop had only one vehicle, an out-of-state Fiesta that looked like it had a blown tire up on the racks.

I felt for the guys in the shop. They knew what had happened wasn't my fault, but at the same time, they couldn't help but blame me just a little bit. After all, Chris had been my friend, and I'd been the one to take him down, which indirectly hurt them. Sure, it's a side of people that we don't like to talk about, but I didn't fault them for it. The negative press would most likely cost them their jobs.

I found Hank Lake in his office, sipping a cup of coffee and looking about twenty years older than I had seen him the week before. The sales manager was with me, mostly to make sure there wasn't a scene. It was the last thing anyone needed. "Mr. Lake? I just came by to turn in my resignation and to hand in my keys."

Hank looked up and held out his hand, his fingers trembling as I handed over the keys. "Also, sir, um, I'm not sure how to do this, but

219

this other key is to the apartment in the Mayfair Tower. It's only for the main door. I don't have a deadbolt key."

I set it on the desk and pushed it closer, Hank's hand recoiling as if the metal were poisonous. The sales manager shifted from left foot to right, not sure what to say or do, and looking like he wanted to be somewhere else at the moment.

Hank swallowed and looked up at me for the first time. "Thank you, Bell. I know that it'd be impossible for you to come back to work here, but . . . I'm sorry. Chris is family, but what he did was wrong."

"You have nothing to apologize for, Mr. Lake. Neither of us recognized what Chris was up to, and I spent years closer than a brother with him. I'm just glad that it's over now."

Hank sighed, then looked at me. "So what now?"

"Take care of your family," I said. "If it were me, after the blow this causes, I'd sell the group, or at least rebrand it. Take the money and make a nest egg for the next generation. As for Chris . . ."

"He'll stand on his own," Hank said with only a hint of venom. "He gets no help from me. I've got two kids of my own to protect."

I nodded. "Then I guess this is it. I'm sorry it didn't work out, Mr. Lake."

Hank stood up and offered me his hand. He may have been hurt, his faith in himself and in his own perceptions shattered, but he was a true man. We shook, and Hank tried to smile. "You're a good man, Dane Bell. Don't ever let anyone tell you different."

\* \* \*

A few days later, I went to the McCamish Pavilion with Brittany, dressed in a suit that I still felt uncomfortable in. Brittany was on my arm, holding a video camera like a young parent at a kindergarten or something.

"If Patrick can't be here in person, I'm going to make sure he can at least see the video," she whispered to me. We had good seats and could see the whole stage where the ceremony would take place. "And stop fidgeting."

"Sorry," I muttered, then laughed. "I guess now, you have someone else you have to teach the social rules to other than Abby?"

Brittany blushed slightly, then patted my arm. "Maybe. It's just a bit of a habit. And if my stepdaughter is going to see you, I'm going to do my best to make sure you're a good influence."

"By the way, they're webcasting this thing too," I said as I looked at the program. "Didn't you know?"

Brittany nodded and adjusted the camera just a bit on its tripod. "I don't care. This is for posterity. Do you think I'm too uptight?"

I thought about it a bit, reflecting that for a woman who I had literally kicked to the floor less than a week earlier, she and I had come to find a common ground rather quickly. Though if it wasn't for a near tragedy, I don't know if that would have been the case. It's weird how it works like that. As we still had some time before the ceremony started, I took my time before answering. "I think you have good intentions. But I do think that the idea of them fitting in with the culture club has pretty much sailed. As for me, you could work with me for the next thirty years, and I still wouldn't fit in. No matter how I talked or acted, one look at my tats and I'd be an outcast."

Brittany thought, then made a sound that was half-laugh, half-sigh. "I guess you're right. Still, if Patrick wants it, I'll keep doing my best to open doors for him. And I'll at least drag Abby to at least one social event a year.

The graduation ceremony itself was actually pretty long and tedious, a lot different from the ones I'd attended before. Then again, my high school graduating class was only a hundred and thirty-five people, and graduating Basic Training was quick as well. Both of those ceremonies could have been started, completed, and probably cleaned up in the amount of time it took for Georgia Tech to graduate the five thousand students who were scheduled to walk the stage that day.

The students walked the stage according to a complex system that left me baffled, until I finally had to lean over to Brittany for help. "When is Abs walking again?"

"She's still got a while."

There was one disruption, when during the College of Engineering's ceremony, Shawnie was announced. She had just been released from the hospital that morning, just in time to make the ceremony. As she made her way across the stage, *summa cum laude*, a wave of applause broke out. She was shocked, but recovered and stood tall, waving to her supporters as she crossed the stage to shake hands with the Dean of the College before walking off stage.

"I underestimated that girl. Abby was right about her," Brittany commented.

When Abby walked, she paused to hug Shawnie when she came off stage before retaking her seat, and the ceremony continued. I had to admit I tuned most of it out, nodding off about halfway through the College of Liberal Arts and having to be woken up with a polite pat on the arm in time for the final playing of the alma mater.

Outside, in the craziness that was the post-ceremony group celebration, I found Abby and Shawnie hugging and exchanging farewells, with lots of people in their graduation robes. Seeing me, Abby ran over, jumping into my arms and an embrace. "I saw you up there," she said, kissing me with a wet smack. "Thanks for staying awake through my part at least."

"How could I not?" I asked with a grin, spinning her around before setting her down. "Although I know you're going to be doing the same thing in a few years again anyway when you get your Masters."

"And what about you?" Abby asked with a grin. "You could do a lot of things if you set your mind to it."

I raised an eyebrow thoughtfully. Me, college? Until I met Abby, I would never have thought of it. "I don't know about that one."

Shawnie finished shaking hands with a professor and came over. She seemed in a good mood, but I wondered how long it would be before the vivacious, wisecracking woman who'd impressed me with her wit and her insight the little bit we talked came back. I didn't know the extent of the details of what she'd been through, and honestly, I didn't want to know. But she seemed to be doing okay, and that's all that mattered. "How're you doing, Shawnie?"

She pointed with her chin, where a small group stood looking at us. "My family's here, so I'm doing okay," she said with a smile. "Dane, I haven't had the chance before, but let me just say thank you."

I shook my head, holding up my hands. "I should have been faster, Shawnie. Trust me, I think about that every minute."

She nodded, then shrugged. "We move forward, big boy."

"So what are your plans?" I asked, putting my arm around Abby's shoulder. A well-wisher came by, greeting Abby and Shawnie as they passed, and Shawnie paused before answering.

"I'm going to take a month or so," She finally said. "Then I think I'm going to head out West, get a jump on settling in."

"In the meantime, you know that I've got all the time in the world on my hands," Abby said. "Maybe a girl's weekend out somewhere?"

"As long as there are no lakes involved, I'm fine with that," Shawnie said. Someone in her family called her name, and she turned and waved. "All right, guys, I have to get going. Family party and all. I'll give you a call tomorrow or something."

As she walked away, I looked at Brittany, who was still smiling broadly. "So, how about the three of us changing clothes and getting over to the hospital? I bet Patrick wants to see that video as soon as possible."

Brittany nodded and patted her camera bag. "Sounds good. I'll drive."

## Chapter 19

## Abby

I was barely able to contain my excitement when Daddy came home, assisted up the steps by Brittany and the occupational health nurse who'd been hired to help him during his rehab protocol. Monica was a former Marine drill sergeant who'd gotten into occupational health after an injury cut her time in the Corps short. She was tiny, just over five feet tall, but built like a truck with a ripped six-pack that rivaled Dane's. I'd met her one time before when she came over to stake out her room, as she'd be living with us for the next month.

"We're running out of guest bedrooms," Brittany said in a good-natured complaint. "Pretty soon, Abby, we're going to be kicking you out to live on your own."

"I guess she can move in with me then," Dane teased as he helped him down into his easy chair. "Since you can't chase me off right now."

"I can still use a shotgun," Daddy growled in good humor. "Besides, I bet that Monica could kick your ass. I always heard Marines were tougher than Airborne."

"We'll settle that at some point," Dane laughed, looking over at her.

We got Daddy settled, and Dane gave me a look that I'd become familiar with over the past few days. "I think Dane and I will take a walk on the back forty," I said, getting up off the couch. "We won't be gone long."

"Okay," he said, leaning back and getting comfortable. "But when you two get back, I'd like to talk with you both about some things I've been thinking about during my time in the hospital."

Dane and I left, heading out the back of the house. While Dane had been living with us for over a week, we hadn't spent a lot of time together alone. I'd needed my time to recover, after all. I'd spent a lot of time with my own thoughts, although I'd also talked with a counselor as well, something I figured I'd continue for a while longer at least. Now, though, I felt like life was finally getting back to normal. "So what's on your mind?"

Dane just shook his head and took my hand, walking with me through the back yard. We reached the point where the manicured lawn gave way to the natural grass and kept going. "How do you feel now that your dad is home?" Dane asked. "I know you've been looking forward to it."

"I have," I said excitedly, "but I know you've been worried. It's one thing to stay in a man's house with his daughter when there's plenty of room, and Brittany told me this morning she appreciates how much of a gentleman you've been. I have, too, by the way. But now that Daddy's home, you're worried."

"I still have enough saved for that apartment I was looking at before," Dane admitted, "but not much else. I kind of feel like I'm back where I was a few months ago. Although I do have one thing that's better than any job or home."

"What's that?" I asked, pausing. We were close to one of my favorite sites on the property, a field that in summer was filled with wildflowers. Even in the light breeze of the day, I could smell it, but you did have to be very careful about the fire ants. They liked that field too.

"I have you," Dane said. "And in all honesty, I don't ever want to let you go."

"I love you too," I answered. "I know we haven't been together long, but everything seems so right."

"Good," Dane said, taking my hand. "Because I was kind of hoping—after we go back, that we could tell your father that I asked you to marry me, and that you said yes."

"Is that what you call a proposal?" I asked, trying hard to hide my joy.

"I love you," Dane said simply, pulling me into his arms. "During my time in prison, I've learned if you want something, you'd better not waste any time. If you want it, go get it. Now, I'm not saying we go get married tomorrow. We can give it some time, but the heart wants what the heart wants."

It was my turn to wrap my arms around Dane, pulling him down for a deep kiss in the summer sunshine. "Is that a yes?"

"Oh, that is certainly a yes," I said. "But we really should get Daddy's blessing first. You know, me being traditional and all."

* * *

When we got back a half hour later, Daddy saw it first, probably from the look in my eye. "You know, I hoped you would've waited until after I said what I had to say."

"Sorry, Mr. Rawlings," Dane said. "I just couldn't let a good thing go."

He sat up, and with the help of Monica, struggled to his feet. "I didn't expect you to move this quickly. So I take it you said yes?"

"Yes, Daddy," I said, pausing while Brittany clapped in joy, "but we also wanted to have your blessing."

He came over and looked Dane in his eye. Sizing him up, Daddy stood nearly eye to eye with him, pausing before looking at me, a small smile on his face. "You know, for so long, it was just you and me. Then I found Brittany, and I knew the day would come that you would also want to find someone of your own. I have to say, this isn't how I expected it would be, but I love you, baby girl."

"I love you too, Daddy," I said, taking Dane's hand. "I always will."

"Which is why I have to say, in response to your request for my blessing . . . no." Daddy turned and made his way back over to his chair, sitting down carefully.

"What?" I cried, tears in my eyes. "Why?"

He grinned and laughed, unable to contain his humor. "Oh, I got you, didn't I?"

I blinked, stunned. "What?"

I looked at him, anger replacing my hurt. "You joke?"

Daddy held up his hands defensively. "Now, Abby, I'm sorry, it was just a quick one. I'd be happy to give you both my blessing . . . when you've earned it. In that, I'm being serious."

"And how would I do that?" Dane asked, his voice heavy with threat and repressed anger. "Haven't I done enough?"

"Oh, you've done enough to prove you're a good man, and that you care for my daughter. Of course you have," Daddy said, smiling. "But I've always been a father who has thought the world of my daughter, and to be honest, while I'm perfectly willing to accept that she won't be marrying a society boy, I do expect her husband to have a job. So, before I give you my blessing, there are a few things you need to do. First, you're going to have to enroll in college."

"I . . . I don't think I'd qualify any longer," Dane said, stupefied. I heard in his voice the surprise at some of his own thoughts that he'd shared with me reflected in Daddy's statement, but he was still taken aback. "I mean, I'm nearly thirty."

"Oh, I can pull a few strings. You won't be in Georgia Tech like Abby, but I can get you into SCAD, the Savannah College of Art and Design. I did a lot of the recent renovation work on their student housing, and I've maintained a good relationship with the Dean. She owes me a favor or two. I'm sure you can find something there that interests you. Brittany told me that you were reading a book on famous architects a while back, and well . . . I was thinking perhaps Rawlings Construction might want to become Rawlings Construction and Design in a few years," Daddy said.

"Of course, I understand your financial situation, so you'll be going under a work-study program. You maintain a certain average, and I'll take care of the rest. You'll work as a management intern at Rawlings Construction. It's not much, but it beats sweeping floors at Lake Auto."

"That's very generous of you, sir," Dane said. "I don't really know what to say."

"Oh, it's not going to be all fun and games," Daddy said with a chuckle. "I plan on working you very hard. But I think you'll handle it fine."

I couldn't help it. I laughed, seeing the genius and the generosity in Daddy's plan. I hugged Dane's arm, looking up at him. "What do you say? Think you can go back to school?"

Dane only had to think for a second. "Damn right I can. One thing, though—does that mean we can't get married until I graduate? I mean, I planned on waiting a while, but not years."

"Oh, no," Daddy said, leaning back. "Whenever y'all think the time is right. Just that my blessing won't be conferred until after your first day of classes. So should I have Brittany give a call to SCAD, or do you need to think it over?"

Dane shook his head and looked at Brittany, his eyes eager and glimmering with excitement. "Can you call them now?"

* * *

After a celebratory dinner in which Daddy granted his approval, if not yet his blessing, to our engagement, Dane and I were alone in the living room.

We sat on the couch, me leaning against him. I still felt thunderstruck, and I was sure I'd had a goofy smile on my face the whole time. "Pinch me."

"Hmm?" Dane asked, rubbing my shoulder. "I wasn't sure I heard that correctly."

"I asked you to pinch me," I said with a small laugh. "Because I'm still not sure I'm awake."

"Well, you're talking, and I know I'm awake, so I'm pretty sure you're awake," Dane answered. He kissed my temple, pausing to inhale the scent of my hair and to whisper in my ear. "But I'm happy to pinch you. Any place you prefer to be pinched?"

I chuckled and rubbed his chest, leaning against him. "For sure, that comes later. I feel a bit strange about it, though."

"Because of what happened at the lake?" Dane asked, immediately stiffening and giving me space. "Sorry, I got caught up in the moment."

"No, silly," I answered, getting onto my knees on the couch and kissing him. "I feel strange because of being here and how mortified I'd be if Brittany or Daddy walked in on us."

"They don't seem like the type that'd cheer us on or give suggestions," Dane joked in reply, kissing me back. "Your dad has warmed up to me a bit, but he'd still probably contemplate on grabbing his shotgun."

His humor was exactly what I needed to relax enough to do what we both wanted to do for too long. Dane pulled me into his lap, humming in appreciation at the slick texture of my nylon sleep shorts. "You wear those every night?"

"Most of the time," I said, my hips rubbing back and forth across the hardness growing beneath me in his pants. "Except in the winter. Then I might wear flannel pants."

"Well then, I guess we're going to have to make sure our home is warm year-round," Dane replied, reaching down and cupping my ass. "Because this is far too good of a feeling to give up because of some damn weather."

I had to agree, as the slick fabric let his strong hands roam as he pulled me in closer, our lips meeting softly with long, gentle caresses. I could feel the desire within him, but he restrained himself, his hands more tender than he had ever been. I leaned back, breaking our kiss, and stroked his hair. "Dane, you don't have to hold back," I whispered, kissing his forehead. "There's nothing I want more than to make love with you right here, right now."

Dane's feral grin thrilled me, and he fiercely pulled me into him, our lips crushing together as he gave vent to his passion. He pushed my thin t-shirt up and over my head, freeing my breasts at the same time. Holding me like I weighed just a feather, he feasted upon my nipples, alternating from left to right in a chaotic pattern that never let my body adapt, each switch bringing fresh waves of pleasure through my body and shooting all the way to my pussy. *"Dene . . ."*

"Abs," Dane mumbled between my breasts, looking up at me.

I shifted back, slipping down Dane's thighs slightly in order to be able to find the clasp of his pants. His cock was already hard and hot under my fingers as I undid the clasp and pulled the zipper down. Dane jumped in my hand as I reached into his underpants to take his long, thick cock out and hold it between us, pulsing with life and hunger.

"I want to ask you something," I said, leaning in and kissing him again. "And you can give me an honest answer. It won't change a thing about what we're about to do."

"What?" Dane asked, his breath hissing from between his teeth as I stroked him while my breasts pressed against his chest.

"What do you think about having children?" I asked, sitting up and wedging his cock between us. My pussy was aching, needing him inside me, but I had to have the answer to this question all of a sudden. "In general, I mean."

"Well, I think we'll need at least ten months," Dane teased, sliding his right hand inside my shorts to caress the skin of my ass again. "Seriously, though, I think having a baby with you would be the greatest thing in the world, and if it happens, I'd welcome it. But I think after your schooling would be best."

I smiled and reached down and pushed the leg of my shorts and panties to the side. There would be time for gentleness later, but my initial urge for tenderness had been replaced by the white-hot passion of going so long without Dane. For a week, we'd been in the same house, spending time together but not being intimate as he gave me time and space to let my mind heal. Now, the slowly building fire inside me was at nuclear levels, unable to be contained. "One more thing."

"What?" Dane grunted as I took his cock in my hand again and rose.

"I need you, as powerful and wonderful as you can be." I chuckled as I lowered myself onto him. Dane's cock would forever be a wonderful experience, each time leaving me feeling like a newly discovered virgin, thrilled and a bit frightened by the first sensations of his huge cock spreading me open, stretching me and filling every nook and cranny of my body.

Dane lifted me up and down on his magnificent tool, letting my body adjust and stretch until the fear was replaced with wave after wave of delicious pleasure, my breath catching in my throat every time my body lowered itself onto his shaft. To add to the feeling, the position of our bodies meant that my clit dragged over his stomach with each movement, making me nearly insensate. I was getting pleasure with each up and down stroke, never ceasing, just building.

My eyes drifted closed. I couldn't focus any longer, when I suddenly felt a sharp pinch on my right nipple, painful and arousing at the same time. My eyes flew open to see Dane grinning up at me. "What? You did ask me to pinch you earlier."

Dane wrapped his arms around my hips and stood up, still impaling me on his huge cock as he laid me down on the living room carpet. Pulling out, he stretched his arms and legs, then laid down beside me, a confident grin on his lips. "Now I can move some. Turn over."

I couldn't help but obey the loving command in his voice, each tone dripping with desire. When I was on my side, Dane lifted my knee, spreading my legs before he drove forward again, this time mostly from behind, filling me all the way with one sure, mind-blowing stroke of his cock. I couldn't help it. I grunted and cried out softly. The hammering beat of his cock drove me wild, my body flushing over and over again with the explosion of pleasure that came from deep inside me. I turned my head, burying my mouth into my forearm to stifle my cries of pleasure.

The only sound I could hear was the rush of my pulse in my ears and the sound of Dane's hips slapping against my ass. Other than the soft whistle of his breathing through his nose, he kept totally silent as my man fucked me hard and fast on the carpet. My pussy clenched around him and my body rippled as my first orgasm shot through me, my teeth clamping down on the meat of my forearm hard enough to leave marks as I moaned and cried out. Dane held me, his cock throbbing inside me. He was so close, letting me ride out my orgasm in my own pace, comforting me and letting me know he would be there.

When the wave passed, I turned and kissed him softly. "You didn't come yet," I said, feeling him still hard and pulsing.

Dane grinned as he readied himself again, pushing inside and sending fresh waves of pleasure up my body. My fingers clutched at Dane's back as he pushed in and out of me, driving me down into the pillow as his body rubbed against my clit. I felt something building inside me in a deeper place, someplace that I'd never felt before. I wasn't sure what it was, but it kept growing, larger and larger, until I was nearly frightened out of my mind. It was too large, I was feeling too much, but at the same time, I couldn't refuse it even if I wanted to.

Somehow, Dane knew what I was feeling. "Let it go," he whispered in my ear. "Same time as I do."

I bit my lip and nodded, untrusting of my voice as he kept pounding into me, strong and confident. I felt him swell, and with a strangled gasp, he thrust into me one last time, his cock erupting. His orgasm triggered an explosion inside me, so strong that I couldn't hold back, burying my mouth into his shoulder and screaming, it was so strong. I tasted the rich, coppery flavor of Dane's blood, and I blacked out for a moment, my mind unable to deal with all of the input at once.

Dane held me, nestling me on his right leg while stroking my hair. "Welcome back," he whispered. "I was wondering if I could sneak you down the hall to your room without someone noticing me carrying you."

"Well, that wouldn't be good, now would it?" I asked, reaching for my t-shirt. "On the other hand, if we walked down the hallway together, we might be quiet enough that you could join me."

Dane smiled and took my hand, stroking it tenderly with his

thumb. "I don't know," he said with a smile. "Your Daddy might still have that shotgun around. And now he's got a Marine, too."

## Chapter 20
### Dane

It was a rarity in Atlanta as snowfall dotted the winter landscape. It was a rare gift to get the day after Christmas, and one that I appreciated. "You're probably one of the few people who aren't freaked out by this," Patrick said to me as I looked out the big glass window of the rented hotel ballroom area. "Think you can get us all home without a problem?"

"Patrick, it's less than a quarter-inch of snow," I said with a light laugh. "I think even you Southerners could drive home in this. The most dangerous thing out there right now is the other drivers, panicking and acting like idiots."

"Never underestimate the ability of mankind to act like idiots," he replied, taking a sip of his whiskey. He was looking remarkably well for a man after his second heart attack. Part of that was due to his month with Monica, I was sure. She'd imbibed a bit of Marine spirit into him, and he took up jogging, working himself up to two miles a day over the ground in the back yard. I'd even paced him once or twice, and he did pretty good for his age. "By the way, congratulations again on the first semester. You did well."

I turned away from the window and took a sip of my own whiskey and soda. "I'll be honest. I was scared stupid for about the first week or so. It was only because of Abs that I was able to get my head out of my ass and recognize that I actually enjoy learning."

"I'd say a 3.2 GPA for your first semester back after a decade off from school is more than cause for celebration," Patrick said. "Come on, let's enjoy the rest of the party. Those from the company who showed up, at least."

"Hey, more for us then," I joked. "You know, besides the bar."

"This is my month's ration of fried foods, so don't make me regret it too much," Patrick joked in reply. We left the entryway and went back into the party, where the place was only about half full. We hadn't expected a big turnout. After all, the party was being held the day after Christmas, but with everything else going on in our lives, it was about the only way to fit it in.

"So you really won't mind that I'm taking a few weeks off?" I asked as we made our way through the room. "I mean, three weeks right after the beginning of the year isn't exactly easy for the company."

"You know, Dane, I've watched you carefully the past six months," Patrick said, stopping about a third of the way across, near a large cake that was shaped like an excavator and festooned with a fondant banner that read *Merry Christmas and Happy New Year, Rawlings Construction.* "And I'll admit that I've been more than a little tough on you. I've given you enough rope to hang yourself more than once, and each time you keep busting your ass and working hard. So let me give you a little bit of advice."

"What's that?" I asked, curious. While I didn't think that he'd ever let me out to dry, I do know that he consciously avoided giving me the rub around the office. He wanted me to stand and become respected on my own, not because I was his daughter's fiancée. It had taken a fair bit of work, but I felt like I was fitting in around the place now and could hold my own with some of the regular workers.

"You're getting married tomorrow," Patrick said, pointing to the table where Brittany and Abby were chatting. Their relationship had grown closer in the past six months, and while I doubted that she would ever call her Mom, Abby had certainly come to understand and appreciate more about Brittany than I think she had in the nearly twelve years prior. "The one thing that I value most, looking at that table now, is the time that I spent not building properties. It's the time I spent playing with my little girl. I'm prouder of the fact I could make Barbie's horse whinny than the fact that I can buy a couple of real horses."

"So you think I should back off?" I asked, incredulous. "After all you've pushed me toward in the past half-year?"

"I think you should work just as hard as you have every moment since they let you out of Leavenworth," Patrick retorted, giving me a half-grin at the end. "Just make sure you're working on the right things, that's all."

One of the company vice presidents came up, wishing us a happy holiday, and I used it as an opportunity to part ways with them. I'd come to admire Patrick, and while our relationship got off to a rocky start, we got along well enough. There was, of course, the unstated but obvious tension as his daughter let him go and became closer to me, but I think every man goes through that when he gets engaged.

I headed over to Abby and Brittany, who were laughing as Abby described in detail our new apartment. We'd moved in just after Thanksgiving, after the neighbors in the first apartment complex we'd tried had turned out to enjoy partying a bit too much for our tastes. "Yeah, I know it's still nowhere near what I had at home with you and Daddy, but it's ours," Abby said as I approached. I figured she was telling Brittany about our upstairs neighbors, who had a slightly disturbing habit of turning their nightly yoga sessions from Iyengar to Tantric, if you know what I mean. Still, better than listening to Flo Rida all weekend long. "We figure it'll keep us going for a while though. At least until I finish my Masters."

"You ladies make this party a lot better looking than any decoration or band could," I greeted them as I came within greeting distance. Abby got up and we kissed, laying her head on my shoulder. "Hey, Abs. You miss me?"

"Not too much," she teased me, rubbing my chest. "Just enough that I can't wait until tomorrow."

"Oh, you can wait another few hours," Brittany laughed, sipping at her champagne. "After all, it isn't like in my parents' day when the couple would have to spend every night apart until the wedding ceremony."

"Good for us, then." Abby laughed. She reached down to the table and took a sip of her ginger ale, something I'd noticed earlier. Abby had never been a big drinker, but then again, neither was I. I used to be, but I'd seen firsthand what nastiness alcoholics could do. In the apartment, we didn't have any alcohol at all other than a bottle of Malbec that we'd been given as a gift for moving in. "Say, babe, are you sure you'll be good for picking Shawnie up from the airport tomorrow?"

"Yeah, this is my last one," I replied, taking the final sip and setting the glass down on the table. "I don't want to have my nuptials marred by a hangover or anything."

Brittany smiled in approval and finished her glass of champagne as well. "A wise decision. Well, you two enjoy yourself. I need to powder my nose, as the saying goes."

She left us, and I led Abby closer, away from the table, and took her out to the dance floor. The live band wasn't the best in town, but even a second-rate band in a city like Atlanta can beat the pants off anything a lot of other places can offer. We found an empty spot on the dance floor and I pulled her into my arms. "Think of it as practice for tomorrow."

"You know, I think Brittany is expecting at least a little bit of Viking tomorrow with all of that Norse stuff you talk about," Abby said as we danced. "She's going to be highly disappointed."

"Well, I guess I could rip off my shirt, grease myself up, and try to wrestle a bear, but those are kind of hard to find this time of year," I joked. "I guess she'll have to settle for the roasted meats and maybe a song or two. You know I just take it in stride anyway."

"I know. It's why I love you so much," Abby said. "Enjoying the party?"

"Better than listening to the Washingtons upstairs," I replied. "Trying to watch *The Charlie Brown Christmas Special* while they were having sex was not the experience I was hoping for."

"We've kind of given them a concert or two as well," Abby reminded me. "Or did you forget Monday night?"

"How could I?" I chuckled. We turned on the floor, moving in gentle circles, not really following any one pattern but just moving together. "Hey, Abs, I don't want to pry, but you seem to be a bit off tonight. Worried about tomorrow?"

"No," Abby replied. "I'm excited, yes, but not worried. Why?"

"I just noticed you're only hitting the ginger ale. You don't think we'll get too drunk and oversleep, do you?"

Abby leaned back, her honey blonde hair shimmering in the soft light, her blue eyes twinkling like twin sapphires, and laughed, long and loud. If it hadn't been a party, or if the music had been softer, she would have garnered a lot of attention, but as it was, she barely registered. When her laughter was over, she pulled my head down and kissed me. "I'm not worried about that at all," she whispered in my ear after the kiss was broken. "I wanted to wait until we were alone tonight, but I have a late Christmas gift for you."

"Oh? What's that?" I asked, flummoxed. We hadn't exchanged too many gifts, so a late one seemed strange.

"You get to find out in about nine months," Abby whispered, pulling back to look me in the eyes. "Merry Christmas . . . *Daddy*."


The End...


Thank you for reading. If you enjoyed this, check out my other books at www.LaurenLandish.com

xoxo

## About The Author

Lauren Landish is a Bestselling Author of Romance. Writing has always been her first love and she's happy to write for women who are thirsty for a little heat in the bedroom!

Lauren is a former resident of the sunny land of California, but now resides across the country in North Carolina with her boyfriend and her pet mini schnauzer.

Visit Lauren's Website at: http://www.laurenlandish.com